THE STARDUST COLLECTION

DAWN BLAIR

MORNING SKY STUDIOS

Cover and layout copyright © 2020 by Morning Sky Studios
Cover design by Dawn Blair/Morning Sky Studios
Cover art copyright © Deepgreen | Dreamstime.com, © Andreus | Dreamstime.com, © Andreiuc88 | Dreamstime.com, © Chaiyas | Dreamstime.com, © Albund - Dreamstime.com, © Dawn Blair, © Mikel Martinez De Osaba | Dreamstime.com, © Dwnld777 | Dreamstime.com, and © Alena Akanovich | Dreamstime.com

Morning Sky Studios
PO Box 5422
Twin Falls, ID 83303
Visit us at www.morningskystudios.com

ALSO BY DAWN BLAIR:

Onesong

Tangled Magic

Walk the Path

Sacred Knight

Quest for the Three Books

Manifest the Magic

To Birth a Destiny

History of a Dead Man (companion novella)

Prince of the Ruined Land

The Missing Thread

The Unicorn and the Secret (companion novella)

The Loki Adventures

1-800-Mischief

For Sale, Call Loki

For A Good Time, Call Loki

For More Information, Call Loki

For More Mischief, Call Loki

1-800-CallLoki (Omnibus of novellas 1-5)

1-800-IceBaby

Help Wanted, Call Loki

Wells of the Onesong

Fractured Echo

Fall's Confession

The Doorway Prince

Stardust

Mystery of the Stardust Monk

Alexander's Den

Other short stories

The Last Ant

Broken Smiles

Oxygen

I'm With Cupid

Let's Make a Deal

Tree of Death

Give Up the Ghost

Protective Mythology

By the Numbers

Space Ninjas Aren't Real

Nonfiction

The Write Edit

90 Seconds to Courage

Children's Picture Books

Eggs at Play

EVERYONE COMES HERE EVENTUALLY

ALEXANDER'S DEN

DAWN BLAIR

AUTHOR OF THE ONESONG SERIES

ALEXANDER'S DEN

ALEXANDER'S DEN: A PLACE VERY FEW PEOPLE KNEW ABOUT and even fewer actually ventured into willingly.

Thomis stared at the building, knowing just how cliché the line sounded in his head. But in this case, it was oh so true.

The place wasn't a sketchy dive like one might expect, nor was it posh and only somewhere the exclusively rich went. No, it fit somewhere in-between. Everyone here had a story; some wanted to tell it, and some didn't.

Still, it wasn't where Thomis wanted to be.

The tavern sat at the base of a cliff one would hesitate to call a mountain. It seemed as if wood had merely fallen off the hardscrabble rocks above and piled up into a shape that resembled a building, except that there were no trees on the arid landscape.

Thomis took one last deep breath of the dry air as he stared at the structure. He shook the dry canteen at his side, wishing he had just one more drop to swallow and loosen up his voice before he went inside. It had been a long, hot walk, and all along the way he'd been asking himself why he was making the trek. Would it be worth it?

He adjusted the thick strap of the bag he wore across his chest so the weight of it would hang on a different part of his shoulder and give the other a chance to rest. A breath of sand whipped across the desert and threatened to spew grit in his eyes. It seemed almost as if the larger universe threw rocks at him to tell him he shouldn't be here and keep him away.

With gentle pressure, he pushed at the throbbing spot on his head where a deep ache had settled. Hopefully once he got inside and out of the sun, it would subside.

The hinges creaked in a long, yowling announcement as he pulled the door open. Thomis felt as if every eye in the room was on him as soon as he walked in. He knew that wasn't true since most people in here wanted to keep their heads down and out of trouble. Still, he felt as if he was being watched, especially by long-time regulars who might have their questions. He looked at the slats of the wooden floor as he traversed to the counter on the other side of the room. The bartender saw him walking through the smoke and moved to intercept him.

"Do ya for something?" the bartender asked. Thomis didn't know the man. Strange. Alexander wasn't known to have much employee turnover. Very few made it out after being employed at the Den. It was a lifetime position.

Thomis kept his voice brave. "I need to speak to Alexander."

"That right?"

"Yeah. Yes." Thomis kept his eyes on one particularly black knot in the wood of the counter. It twisted in such a way that made him think that whoever had cut through this piece had had a heck of a time doing it. The glossy sheen made Thomis think that the bar must have been recently replaced.

"No one speaks to Alexander."

Now Thomis raised his eyes and met the bartender's gaze. "Unless they are on the list. Check it. I'm on the list."

The bartender rolled his eyes as if to say, "Yeah, sure you are," but he took two steps to the side and pulled out a thick board with a rusty nail sticking out of it, which split a piece of parchment with a wide hole. "Your name?"

"Rastin. Thomis Rastin."

The man's lips moved as he scrolled with his finger down the paper and read each name. Thomis could tell there weren't nearly that many names actually written on the list, but then he saw the bartender's yellow eyes. It made Thomis' heartbeat quicken. The instinct to back slowly away nearly overtook him.

The bartender blinked before looking up. His eyes once again looked human. "Don't see your name on here."

For a moment, Thomis thought about threatening the bartender. Fortunately, he quickly remembered what he was pitting himself against if he did. He made the decision not to make the challenge. "I don't suppose Alexander ever makes any exceptions, does he?" Thomis smiled, hoping that some of his Welsh charm would help.

The bartender didn't look amused. "Never," he said with a roll of his sneering lips.

"I use to be his partner. We built this place together."

"Sure ya did."

Thomis backed away from the counter, nodding as he went. "Okay then. Well, I was certain me name would be on that list. Guess he wouldn't be caring about the dragon egg I found either then, would he?"

The man's eyes narrowed suspiciously. "Dragon egg?"

"I can always find another buyer," Thomis tried hard not to smile, "if Alexander's not interested in it."

The bartender's eyes narrowed on him, but Thomis didn't

care. Rather, he put on the goofiest smile he could muster. A real Welesh grin, the type to make the girls in his village swoon at what a lovable oaf he could be. He lifted his eyebrows, waggling them just for good measure.

Thomis didn't think the man was falling for it.

"I'll be right back," the bartender said. "You best not be lying about the dragon egg."

"Would I lie about a thing like that to you?" Thomis called after the bartender's retreating back. After the bartender disappeared, Thomis turned, leaned himself against the counter, and crossed his arms over his chest. Now to wait. He had to remain confident that Alexander wanted to see him.

He hoped. It took the remains of his grin off his face along with any cheer in his mood. That made his headache re-establish itself in the front of his skull. He knew the last thing he needed was stress.

He certainly had never planned on coming back here again.

Alexander's Den hadn't changed much. There were still curtained booths where people hid away hoping to gain a moment of privacy for whatever dealings they thought they were getting away with. Sometimes it was a chance for an interlude or a quick affair. Most people didn't want much, only a taste. Thomis had been the facilitator on several of those deals where people wanted to bend the rules but not fully break them. Most people were cowards, feeling naughty by dipping their bare toes in the water but never going for the full skinny-dip.

That had been one of the reasons why Thomis had left and never looked back.

Another had been Alexander's appetites.

Thomis pushed his mind away from that mental trail while looking around the rest of the room to see what had and hadn't changed. The gambling tables were moved from where they once had been placed. Separated even. Now the richer clientele sat on one side, and those hoping to change their fortune assembled in hopeful prayer on the other. On the cupboards behind the bar, the magic monkey still played above the din, banging away on his little drum, yet producing enough sound as if five bards performed. Damnedest thing Thomis had ever seen. Alexander kept it to spare the cost of actually paying people to play. Anything to save a coin.

While the magic monkey was an impressive piece, Thomis knew that Alexander kept the real curios in his back room. Everything out here was just for show.

"Alexander says ya can come on back. He says he's been waiting for ya," the bartender said.

Thomis couldn't help his smirk. "Told you he was expecting me. Me name should've been on that list."

"Whatever."

He ushered Thomis around the counter; Thomis already knew the way, but why poke the bartender and potentially irritate a dangerous man?

The back room was relatively empty of living beings, save for a couple of older gentleman playing a friendly game of blackjack while sipping wine from long tall glasses which twisted as though the glass itself had had too much alcohol. Each of them wore a black suit, showing they were obviously off-worlders. Respected enough to be invited to Alexander's back room, and they'd been here long enough that the objects around them in the various cabinets no longer struck their awe. Maybe they'd even become regulars here. Thomis nodded with a charming smile at them, then continued after the bartender.

Meanwhile, the leathery wings of several different types of dragons hung from the ceiling. The lights behind them shone through and cast the room into a myriad of diffused colors. Accompanying skulls hung from the walls, several holding candles behind their eye sockets or within the holes that were once the dragons' nostrils. Just for kicks and giggles, a couple candles were impaled on the lower front teeth of a skull with a major underbite. Necklaces with huge gemstones or strands of beads and feathers hung from the mouths of other skulls, blood of their former owners still splattered across the objects.

The bartender stopped while Thomis walked slowly along. When Thomis realized that the man waited for him, he grinned, "Just checkin' things out."

"Shocks everyone the first time. But that wouldn't be you... his former partner who helped him build this place."

Thomis withheld the snort he felt rising along with the glib words he wanted to add about the bartender disbelieving Thomis' story. This was far from his first time in this room. "Just checkin' it out," he repeated softly.

The bones displayed at the back room became more humanoid as Thomis followed the bartender though a door which exited into a mountain tunnel. Many who first saw it surmised that it must be a natural tunnel to a cave. Thomis knew otherwise; he'd worked this mine before Alexander came along, bought the mountain, and closed the mine. Well, it hadn't been Alexander doing the legwork but rather just providing the funds behind it all. It still galled Thomis for the part he had played in it.

Another trip down memory lane he didn't wanted to take right now, and Thomis narrowly avoided the turnstile that lead off in that direction.

As they went deeper into the carved tunnel, the man ahead of him seemed to walk deliberately slow, as if he were forewarning Thomis.

"Alexander's Den is living up more and more to its name," Thomis laughed. "This is what I expected when I walked in."

"Yeah, it gets real sometimes," the bartender said.

The clinking of coin falling through a metal pipe drew Thomis' attention overhead to the drainage system that ran near the ceiling. Score, he thought to himself almost as a reflex. Then he remembered that he'd get none of the take heading down the pipe.

"Falling rock," the bartender lied. "Keep your head down."

"Yeah, sure," Thomis muttered. For only a few minutes longer he would have to keep up this pretense. Just long enough to get to Alexander.

Diamonds sparkled in the stone walls as the temperature began to rise. Thomis tamped his forehead with the long sleeve of his shirt. "Sure gets hot in here, doesn't it?"

The bartender smiled wryly back over his shoulder. "You're about to find out why."

Thomis knew the bartender was still smirking as they charged ahead.

The bartender stopped at a doorway illuminated by two tall lanterns. "Here you are," he said with a flourished wave toward the door.

"No introduction?" Thomis mocked.

The bartender sneered, "If you need an introduction, you're in the wrong place." Bumping Thomis' shoulder as he went, the bartender started back down the way they had come in.

Thomis watched the bartender go until the man moved out of his peripheral vision. He turned his attention back to the door, where just beyond Alexander would be waiting alone.

Thomis entered a vast hollow filled with light reflecting off glistening gemstones embedded in the cavern walls. In the center of the room, a pile of books reached toward the ceiling. As Thomis walked across the floor, he saw that it was still the same thick glass that had always been there, though it was now beginning to yellow from age and heat. Beneath, he saw the spines of so many books that he felt like he was walking on library shelves that had been knocked over. The truth wasn't too different. All those books lined up were the collection that he and Alexander had built up over the ages.

But what Thomis didn't see was Alexander.

He crept forward, rolling only his eyes to check the ceiling of the cave above him. He didn't want to look up and risk Alexander surprising him. Nor did he want Alexander to drop down on him.

He made his way to an edge where the floor quit being glass and was once again rock.

"You do not bring me books!" A head began to slowly rise from the pile, sending an avalanche of paper toward the glass floor. "What do you seek from me where you do not first pay my price?"

"I come bearing something I hope you will find much more valuable than a book." Thomis thought Alexander's head looked much smaller than it had the last time they had spoken. Had Alexander aged that much?

Alexander's long head swung toward Thomis as two long legs ascended the pile. Thick, black claws struck more books and sent them sliding down the pile. "Storyteller!"

"Hello, Alexander," Thomis broached carefully.

Alexander's eyes narrowed even as the black slits in the center of the yellow iris dilated into a diamond shape. "My barkeep said you were here; I didn't believe it. Figured someone used your name in order to come make a request of me. Why do you enter my presence again?"

Thomis knew his moment was now or never. He ran his tongue over his lips, not sure if it helped in this heat, glanced to the floor, and took a careful step forward toward the dragon. "Because I have been hearing tales which I thought you might like to know about."

"Are they good stories?" Alexander seemed wary.

Thomis risked another fateful step forward. "I am daring to return after all this time. What do you think would make me set foot before you again?"

Alexander waited a moment, thinking. "A dragon egg. Yes, least that much of your tale has been spoken. But there's more too, isn't there?"

"I have many tales from across different lands." Thomis hated giving away his bargaining chip, but what else could he do. The universe was in chaos. He had to get Alexander to listen. "Most of them don't have happy endings."

Alexander turned and climbed down the backside of the pile of books. He came around the side and Thomis saw that Alexander was much smaller than the last time he'd seen the dragon. Further bad news.

Worst still, Alexander seemed tired. The dragon had never before been without incredible energy. Now, his eyes drooped, pulling down at the far corners slightly. Even his scales had gone dull, barely a lackluster sparkle now. Without a smile, the solemn mood followed the dragon as if he wore a blanket tied around his neck. "Then you may indeed bring me a good story," Alexander said.

Thomis hadn't anticipated that reaction from the dragon.

"Come now, Thomis," Alexander said, lopping toward him with slow paces full of the aches and pains of his age. Yet the dragon hardly seemed any larger than when they had first met. "We both grow weary of the constant struggles that go on out there."

"You can't tell me the people's lives matter that little to you. You've never been one to be sentimental about humans, but you love their adventures. Those struggles are the center of your imaginings."

"Stories of courage and heart. Not tales of slaughter and mayhem," Alexander replied angrily.

That much had been true.

This was different.

"You've gotten old. Your hair has gray in it and your skin has started to wrinkle," the dragon grumbled. Alexander turned and started walking around the pile away from Thomis. At least, even while time had weakened the dragon, Alexander still had the strength to not drag his tail behind him. It lifted a couple feet off the ground and swayed back and forth with Alexander's lumbering pace.

"I'll stay." Thomis had a hard time not shouting the words. His chest felt tight. He hadn't expected it to be this difficult. "I won't leave you again. We can change things, make them the way they should be."

"Really?" the dragon sneered back at him.

"Yes."

"I've been without your stories for a long time. I've found others to occupy my time." Alexander swung his head toward the pile of books.

"They obviously don't nourish you enough though. You need more substance."

"Better to deal with some malnutrition than a traitor."

The words stung Thomis, though he knew he should have expected this reaction from Alexander. From the dragon's perspective, Thomis had betrayed him. Certainly, his last words to Alexander hadn't been kind.

"So, is the dragon egg a true story, or just a ploy to let me allow you in here rather than roasting you where you stand?" Alexander asked, lumbering around to face Thomis again.

"Oh, the egg is real," Thomis smiled. "It's small, but it's got to be an imagination dragon. We can set things right."

"So, you don't even know its parentage. You come here to bargain with only a possibility on your side?"

"A minor, technical detail. That's why I've come to you,

you see? I want you to identify it. I want you to see if I'm correct about it."

Alexander sneered, his muzzle wrinkling fiercely. "Which is why you agreed to stay? You knew that if it is another imagination dragon, I would take it in and protect it. You want two imagination dragons under your thrall, don't you, storyteller?"

As much as Thomis hated the ethical implication of Alexander's words, Thomis knew his actions didn't speak to the contrary. "Yes, Alexander, entertaining is what I do. If I hold the imaginings of one, or two, or six dragons, what does it matter?"

Alexander made another turn and paced the other direction. "But we're not just dragons, now are we? We are special births, dragons born for a purpose, and we dream up the universe. You have already tainted that! Because of you, I had to stop creating worlds."

"Which is why I'm coming back to you," Thomis pleaded. "Don't you understand? I know it's my fault: the corruption, your worlds falling into chaos and despair. I'm sorry for what I said to you, how I hurt you, but I wanted my own adventures. You craved new stories all the time, something to feed your imagination, but I had lost touch with the real world. I had to go away."

"Run away," Alexander corrected.

"Yes, I ran away! I left you! No, I abandoned you. I get it. I regret it. Don't you think I sodden drank myself into a stupor many nights over what I did? I saw the devastation and I tried to stop it. No matter how many stories I went out and told, no matter how many lives I tried to brighten, no matter how many endings I changed, I couldn't weave my tales fast enough. No one wanted to listen. No one cared. The magic was gone and I was too late. It's as if the whole universe is falling apart out there." After he'd said it all,

Thomis felt exhausted, yet relieved. "Storytellers don't save the world."

Alexander silently assessed him for a long moment. "Do you have the egg in the bag?"

Thomis had nearly forgotten all about it. He perked up as he hurried to lift the flap. "Yes, yes me do." Falling into the old Welesh instinctively rather than intentionally putting it on as a charm shocked Thomis a bit and he wondered if Alexander were casting some sort of reveal spell over him to make him truthful. Taking the hardened, sparkling, black shell between his hands, he pulled it from the canvas bag. He could have held the tiny, round egg in one hand, but he feared dropping it. "Saving this egg is literally the last thing I can do to right all the wrongs I've caused."

As Thomis held it up, Alexander took a couple steps closer and turned his head to peer at the egg through his left eye. "Where did you find it?"

"Among some old scrolls I was pulling out of a desecrated library." Thomis knew the description alone would evoke the dragon's memories of being found. He heard Alexander chuckle, but his headache chose to flare at that moment and he pressed his fingers once more to his head as he suppressed a groan of pain. He cradled the egg against him, hoping the throbbing wouldn't make him involuntarily drop it.

"It's a special birth all right," Alexander confirmed, not seeming to notice Thomis' distress. "It looks a bit cold though. It might be too far gone. Or a dud. Why don't you put it down on the floor?"

Thomis kept a careful eye on Alexander as he placed the egg on a section of the floor where it was stone. He wasn't completely certain that he trusted the dragon not to toast him up as well as the egg. Thomis was in Alexander's den, after all. And dragons had long memories, as Alexander had often reminded him.

As Thomis moved carefully back, Alexander began to blow a light stream of warm air toward the egg. Thomis quickly moved to the side, avoiding the intensely heated wind. Still, he couldn't escape how quickly the temperature rose in the cave. The crystals fogged over and darkened the cave slightly.

After a moment, the egg began to rock.

Both Alexander and Thomis gave expressions of shock and amazement to each other.

Sparkles rose off the egg and shimmered in the air as if making its own little glistening cloud.

Alexander stared at it, the corners of his mouth upturned slightly. "It could very well be an imagination dragon. We won't know for certain until the shell really starts to shimmer," he said in a soothed tone. "It certainly isn't a dud."

"How long before it hatches?" Thomis asked.

Alexander took a quick look around, then jutted his head toward the doorway. "Grab one of the sconces outside."

Thomis pulled one of the torch poles out of the slot on the wall beyond the doorway and brought it back inside. He began to lay it down on the rock beside the egg.

"Tip it carefully now," Alexander advised. "Slowly. Slowly. Don't go too fast. You'll smother the flame out."

In regards to smothering, Thomis wanted to tell Alexander that it had been the dragon's own actions which had made Thomis want to flee to begin with. But Thomis held back. There had been several factors and not just that one behind Thomis leaving originally.

Once the egg was backlit, Alexander pressed himself down on the floor beside the egg and began to stare at it. Thomis moved around, seeing the shadow of the creature forming within the egg.

"Look at that," Alexander muttered. "Look at that." He seemed wistfully dreamful.

"So, how long until it hatches?"

"Well, I can see its heart beating, so the scales haven't formed. The wings at this point are just nubs. The shell sparkles, but hasn't taken on the iridescent coat that it will have as it gets close to hatching. I'd say we have long time." Alexander seemed to sag some as the excited energy left him. "There's a monk statue in the back room that needs something to hold. Let's put it on that for a while."

"Seriously, Alexander? You're going to let a statue hold it?" He didn't know if his outrage came from the dragon's idea for taking care of the egg, or that Thomis wouldn't be around to see it hatch.

The dragon stuck his nose up in Thomis' face. "What else am I going to do? Coddle it all the time?"

They stared each other down for a long moment before Thomis scoffed and looked away. "Just like old times, isn't it?"

"Old times," Alexander muttered, turning his head away.

Thomis felt suddenly guilty. He hadn't even been here but a few minutes, and he and Alexander were already up in each other's faces. "Monk statue, back room, right?" he asked.

"Yeah." Sulking, Alexander moved back to his pile of books, leaving Thomis to wonder if the dragon had withered right before Thomis' eyes in the last few moments. Alexander's emaciated body looked as if it hardly had strength enough to care for an egg.

Thomis wandered out through the tunnels and to the back rooms where the men in suits still gambled. The noise had increased, indicating that the stakes of the game had risen. He doubted that lives were on the line, yet. If death weren't a possibility, the perils weren't threatening enough.

Stories, after all, were about characters facing danger.

He chuckled to himself. For a brief moment, it made him happy.

With a sigh, Thomis passed by the tables. He rubbed his

forehead. This was real life, not a story. The drama of real life was never as focused and intentional as in a tale. Stories had purpose. Life, well, that was just life.

No one cared that he walked by.

Storytellers weren't heroes. They didn't save the world. They left that to the heroes of their tales.

In fact, if this were an epic tale, he'd discover that Alexander had made some tragic sacrifice of himself for the egg by the time he got back to the dragon.

Thank goodness this was Thomis' own sad adventure tale.

He found the monk statue sitting in a corner on a low table. Someone had turned him to face the corner as if he'd been placed there because he'd gotten in trouble. Bad monk.

The gamblers began to argue over the cards. Thomis dared to look back at them. One had a black top hat, another sported a mustache clipped not quite evenly. Little details. The tellings of a life.

The stone statue was heavier than Thomis had first thought when he'd tried to pick it up with one hand and he had to lift it with both.

He left the gambling room, taking one final look back at each man sitting around the table. Even though they said nothing to him, choosing only to speak among themselves as if Thomis had never come in the room, he would miss these characters.

Even though the hallways were empty, it rang with the life of memories. Thomis remembered helping Alexander build this place after they'd met in an abandoned library. The imagination dragon had been in dire need of stories. Back then, Thomis had had his own collection of adventures and telling them to Alexander had been wonderful. They'd brought nearly all of the books from the library here, gave them new space and verve. People came from far away to hear Thomis' tales and they brought with them their own which Thomis shared with Alexander. For a while, that had been enough for Thomis. Until...

Until he ran away.

He never imagined he'd be back here.

He lugged the statue into Alexander's lair. Thomis placed the monk statue on the floor and retrieved the egg to set in its hands.

"Perfect," Alexander commented.

Thomis stared at the egg. He felt sorry for it, sitting on the statue as if it were some offering. Had he given up his life for this? Had he returned just to let the monk hold the egg? He still wanted more than this for his existence.

He wanted an adventure. He wanted the dragon to be born. He wanted new stories to tell it. Thomis had to let that all go, put it behind him. He had returned to Alexander's den.

He looked at Alexander, wishing the dragon would hurry up. The hardest part about being a storyteller was waiting for the ones listening to the story to catch up. It felt so lonely being so far ahead.

Alexander noticed Thomis watching him. The dragon sighed. "Now that that's out of the way, do you want tell me why you're really here?"

The dragon's slip to slang meant the formality between them was now gone. Time for serious business between them.

Thomis felt a sad smile move through him and he lowered his gaze to the floor. It allowed him a moment to focus on the statue holding the egg. "Why would you think there was anything else?"

But Alexander didn't have to say. He knew and Thomis knew that just by watching the dragon glancing at the floor too.

"I'm dying," Thomis admitted. The words had to be said. "As it happens to all humans and dragons in their time. Mine just happens to be a little faster these days."

Alexander raised his head, looking hopeful for just a moment before lowering it again. The weight of Thomis' words took the dragon all the way down the glass floor. He kept his head up just a little as he looked toward Thomis. "I take it you've tried everything possible?"

"Yes."

"Even dragon magic?"

Was Alexander hoping that Thomis would beg? "Yes. It's a brain tumor and it's gone too far. They can't operate and it's beyond magical healing. I spent a lot of time digging out mines and handling all sorts of metals, hoping to get enough coin to fund my explorations to climb through dusty, ruined libraries. I guess I shouldn't really have been surprised by the news."

Alexander pouted. "So when you said that you'd stay here with me, it was only because you knew it wouldn't be long."

Thomis hated that it was a comment rather than a question. "I..." What exactly was he planning on saying? He hadn't liked being here, away from the rest of the worlds. He didn't like what his stories had made Alexander weave from the dragon's imagination into the universe. Things would have been better if he'd tried to tell better tales. He always thought the headaches were from him feeling stifled by Alexander's constant need for entertainment. If he'd sought help sooner...

Yes, Thomis said to himself for the millionth time. Yes, Alexander may have been able to help him. If they had caught the progression sooner.

Now, the world would have two hungry imagination dragons to feed and Thomis wouldn't be here to help.

Back to Alexander's question. Had he really come back here to die? He was a storyteller, and they didn't usually go out in some noble firefight with no way out where his name would be spoken as a martyr of freedom for years to come. Certainly he didn't imagine himself telling Alexander some tale and just keeling over while in the middle of the adventure? Maybe he hoped to die peacefully in his sleep while his brain entertained him for a change. Crawling into a dream and never returning seemed like a great way to pass.

It might be more comforting if his dreams hadn't taken a more violent turn of late, usually filled with death. At first, he'd thought it was a reflection of what he'd been seeing out in the universe. Then he realized it was symptomatic of what was going on with him.

Alexander waited, but did the dragon sense the struggle going on within Thomis?

"I think more than anything else I hoped you would have comforting words for me for once," Thomis admitted.

Alexander made a sound somewhere between a scoff and a chuckle; hard to tell with a dragon sometimes. "I forget that you humans are born into this world separated and blinded from your connection to the cosmos. You took on a big challenge when you chose to forget where you came from to enter this world."

How many times had Alexander told him that everything in the universe was connected? How many times had Thomis denied it? He was an individual operating in a realm that constantly tried to take from him or kill him. It had only seemed to get worse as he went out to adventure among the many worlds. Until he started seeing his dreams, his stories, unfolding and realized that Alexander had manifested those visions.

Thomis put a hand to his throbbing head. Confronting Alexander had taken a lot out of him, more than expected.

"Come sit with me," Alexander requested, once again crawling up on the pile of books. He pushed down on the pile as if he could make them have more cushioning while securing them as well.

Thomis exhaled and gave a small shake of his head which

he hoped Alexander didn't notice as he glanced down to the floor and walked toward the dragon. He felt as if he were a prisoner accepting his pending execution. That thought depressed him, yet he took the steps anyway.

He climbed up on the books and settled by Alexander's side as he had so many times before as he went to begin a tale that would allow Alexander to begin imagining his dragon dreams. He felt as if he should speak, but Alexander started first. "Every story we can chose to invite into our lives or not. It can become our friend, or our worst enemy," the dragon said softly. "And when a story ends, we continue on past it, leaving it behind but never forgotten. Especially not if that story has made a mark on us."

"Will I leave my mark on you?" Thomis asked, his eyelids feeling heavy now.

"Undoubtedly." Alexander took in a deep breath and exhaled slowly. "You saved me when you found me in that abandoned library. I'd say that left a mark on many worlds."

Guilt raided him. Thomis didn't want to be here. This was not how he wanted his story to end. There was so much more he wanted to do. Yet he was here. He closed his eyes, allowing himself to relax against the dragon. Alexander would hold him and keep him from falling. "You'll go on though, right, after I'm gone?"

"Somehow."

Silence guided them along an unspoken path through a desolate landscape where neither one of them knew what to say. Until, again, Alexander broke the quiet contemplation between them.

"How about I tell you a story now?" Alexander said. "Once upon a time, a storyteller who longed for adventure walked out among the stars..."

Alexander's Den. This was not where Thomis wanted to be, yet this was the place everyone eventually came.

DAWN BLAIR

MYSTERY
OF THE
STARDUST
MONK

A WELLS OF THE ONESONG STORY

MYSTERY OF THE STARDUST MONK

No one seemed to pay attention to the little monk statue in the garden courtyard anymore.

It had been there so long that it had become part of the scenery. At some point in its history, it had been knocked over and the side of the monk's face chipped off in the accident. The marred stone seemed to keep that portion of it in perpetual shadow. Everyone figured a caretaker had tipped it over and picked it up, placing it back on its unsteady pedestal. But no one knew for certain. And so there rested the little statue of the monk, chipped, broken, but standing tall once more. Just slightly tilted to the left.

In the monk's hand rested a little orb. It shimmered like oil on water and the clarity of the globe changed depending upon the light. It was most beautiful early in the morning on a clear day as the sun was just beginning to rise. Moonhunter knew this, because, for the fifth morning in a row, he stood outside watching it as the sun crested the mountains and the color of the orb went from black to purple, to shimmering with blues and silvers, until finally some pinks and yellows came into the light.

He couldn't say what had originally drawn him here, but it had been in the evening when he and Balthier first arrived. Then, the colors of the orb held more reds and oranges as the sun had set. He awoke early the next morning before Balthier and rushed on outside to see it. Someone else had rambled out that early, heading out to take a walk on the beach and had wondered what Moonhunter was doing standing among the flowers in the courtyard. He wandered over for a closer look.

"That's an ugly statue," the person had said. "You think they'd replace that old broken thing with something prettier."

Moonhunter turned and glared at the man, until the unwanted passerby decided to hurry off in the direction he had originally been going. Most people didn't like Moonhunter's stern look. Other people should keep their opinions to themselves. On the other hand, the man hadn't been entirely wrong. The statue was ugly, especially now that it was broken. However, it wasn't really the statue that had Moonhunter's interest, but rather the orb.

He knelt down before it, trying to look inside the orb. As he got closer, his novihomidrak senses began to ripple in alarm. Not enough to actually activate any of the dragon aspects, but definitely a warning. The chipped monk statue held no power of its own, but the orb did.

Moonhunter extended a talon, short compared to Balthier's, and tapped it against the orb. Little shots of blue and yellowish white lightning reached out to shock Moonhunter, who withdrew before any of the attacks struck him. Of course, he'd been the one to strike first, so the magic probably had a right to retaliate. "I'm sorry," he whispered, not sure why he was talking to the orb, but he had the feeling that it was the right thing to do. He knew when to accept the sensations which came from the Humline about what direction to go. He trusted the natural instinct which flowed within him. And right now, it told him very strongly to apologize to the orb.

The sun rose higher in the sky and the light of the orb changed once more.

With the sound of a door closing behind him, Moonhunter sensed another novihomidrak approaching. Still crouched, he looked back over his shoulder to confirm that Balthier was coming out.

Balthier had indeed risen for the day. He chewed on a thick piece of bread from the kitchens as he approached Moonhunter. "What about that thing has you so fascinated?" Balthier asked.

Moonhunter wished he could answer that question himself, but he couldn't. Instead, he shook his head as he stood up.

"Have you even had a chance to break your fast yet?" Balthier asked.

Moonhunter considered lying. The Humline told him that would be a bad idea. "No, not yet."

"So this thing has been dragging you out every morning before you've even had a chance to care for yourself?"

Moonhunter knew that was true. In fact, he'd been in such a rush to get outside to see it today that he hadn't even relieved himself yet this morning. Nor had he done any of the other things which were his normal morning routine. He'd wanted to get outside and see the orb as first light caught it.

Balthier sighed. "Do you want to know why the orb has your attention?"

Moonhunter did, very much indeed.

"It's made of stardust," Balthier explained. "Most likely gathered from near your home world."

Home world? Moonhunter felt an excited curl through his stomach. "Is that why it attracts me?"

"Most likely." Balthier grunted, but then a light smile

came to his lips. "Ask the owner if you can buy it from him. He might even let you have it. But do it later. We have work to do."

They were on this world to do a job. The mission called and took Moonhunter away from the monk statue.

He never got back to the courtyard to see it again.

When he did see the statue with the stardust orb again many years later, it was no longer in the courtyard. Rather, now it sat in a mansion. Their objective on this world: stop the sale of illegal antiquities by capturing the owner of the mansion, a viceroy who made *mafia* look like a tame word. This time, Moonhunter took a laser blast to the chest for the statue. When he regained consciousness, Balthier had dragged him back to the ship.

Moonhunter woke with Balthier shaking him. Moonhunter glanced around. "The orb? Did I save it?"

"Yeah, you saved the damn thing. You've been out for two days while your body healed though. It could've been a novi-homidrak forged weapon and you could be dead now. I hope you learned a valuable lesson. Some statue is not worth your life."

Moonhunter realized something in Balthier's words, something Balthier wasn't saying. There was more than a hint of disappointment in his words. "And, you weren't able to finish the operation?" He meant it more as a statement because Moonhunter already knew the answer, but it still came out as a question.

"Yeah," Balthier said. The disappointment evident on his face, Balthier turned away. It made Moonhunter realize just how sideways the mission had gone. "They moved the viceroy off world before I had a chance to grab him," Balthier continued. "He escaped while I was trying to save you."

"I'm sorry Balthier," Moonhunter said hoping that Balthier knew how much he meant the words. "I just couldn't let anything happen to the statue. I hope you understand." Balthier turned back and Moonhunter thought he saw smile beneath the man's gruff beard, which he'd been growing out over the last couple missions. "Yeah, I get it. I have a feeling we'll be seeing the damn thing again."

Moonhunter's stomach leapt with excitement. He couldn't wait to see it again. But he knew he'd have to be patient. The Onesong always revealed everything in exactly the right time.

The day came when Balthier and Moonhunter were called before the Dragon Council for yet another world saving mission. Of course, I had found my way into the hallway just outside the Dragon Council's chambers before they even arrived. I watched them walk down the corridor, my heart beginning to pound. I already knew Moonhunter had a special connection to the statue and I knew Balthier's theory: I had been there when Balthier had first proposed it. I had always been in the shadows, waiting, watching.

I stepped into Moonhunter's shadow as he went into the Dragon Council's chambers and the door closed behind them.

The Grand Sapere began by clearing his throat. "Welcome, novihomidraks. We have a new assignment required of you today." The Grand Sapere handed Balthier an envelope.

Novihomidraks accepted their work in a variety of ways, so this did not seem out of sorts for Balthier. He flipped the envelope over and slid his finger beneath the seal, which released with a snapping pop. Balthier pulled out the note card from inside and opened it. A picture floated out. It spun and flipped its way down to the floor where it landed face down on the red carpet. I didn't find it strange at all that Moonhunter was the one that reached for it. He gasped as he looked at the picture. "The stardust monk," he muttered.

He handed the picture off to Balthier, who took it most

absentmindedly while he studied the blank note card more intently. When Balthier finally glanced at the picture, questions filled his eyes. "I don't understand," he said in his gruff voice.

The Grand Sapere shook his head. He had no further details other than the Onesong directing him to assign this undertaking to Balthier and Moonhunter.

"Where is the statue now," Moonhunter asked impatiently. He pointed at the room in the background of the picture. "That's certainly not where we saw it last."

"You've seen the statue before?" the Grand Sapere asked.

Balthier gave his apprentice a most displeased look as if he was not happy about having to explain Moonhunter's injury. "Moonhunter took a laser blast to the chest and was unconscious for two days, all to save this statue." I had always figured that Balthier could be kind of rough, but I had never expected such venom in his words.

"It wasn't like it was a novihomidrak weapon. It was just an ordinary laser pistol. Geez," Moonhunter said.

"You jumped in front of a laser blast in order to save this statue?" the Grand Sapere repeated, hanging his thought in a tone of amazement.

Both Balthier and Moonhunter stared at him as if they hadn't just answered that question.

Balthier turned to Moonhunter. "You are right about that, it's not the same spot."

"It's not the courtyard either," Moonhunter commented.

"So what are we supposed to do?"

I knew I'd better make my move now. I stepped from Moonhunter's shadow, which made both novihomidraks jump. I had been expecting this and I sent out soothing energy before their dragon aspects could appear. "Welcome, gentlemen," I said as I bowed. I remained in a lowered position with my hands outstretched slightly, long enough so that they could see that I had no weapons directed toward them and none even on me. I wanted them to feel perfectly safe, especially since I had surprised them.

"I am the one that has requested your help on this operation," I told him calmly. "I am in need of some novihomidraks."

Balthier looked dubiously at me, his blue eyes narrowing. "What would a ninja want with a couple of novies?"

His question and his tone were not wrong. He was completely correct in neither trusting me nor believing me. Ninjas, as he has called me, rarely needed the help of a novihomidrak. In fact, it was usually my lower classmen of soulcolists which were called in to clean up after a novihomidrak had done his business on the world. Most soulcolists didn't like playing cleanup crew to the novihomidraks. I'd done enough of my own service to know they were generally brutal and harsh. But I had to put my own feelings aside now, as I hoped the novihomidraks would do as well.

I found myself looking toward Moonhunter, knowing that it was really his help above all others that I needed. He was, of course, the one drawn to the monk statue because of the orb. But what I didn't quite understand was how either of the novihomidraks would react if I had told them what the orb really was. "The statue has gone missing." I figured it was best to be straight with them right from the start in so much as I could. "I have been the guardian of the statue for many decades now. It has been an honorary position for me. To say that I have failed in my service does not make me pleased. The statue, or more importantly the orb, must be found and soon. I do hope you realize that for the statue to have been stolen from a ninja who is guarding it means these people are extremely dangerous."

Balthier smiled. He hid it quickly, but not before I had seen it. I knew I had used the right words to enlist the novihomidraks' help. They were hooked. Or at least Balthier was, and therefore, by association, Moonhunter would be to.

"What makes the orb so special, other than the fact that it contains stardust?" Balthier asked. "Why would a ninja be guarding it?"

The way he hesitated when he said stardust, I knew then he was also aware that it was more than just ordinary star-dust. He may have even gathered that it was enlightened star-dust. But I hoped he didn't realize the complete truth about it. If the novihomidraks knew the full details about the orb, especially since I already knew Balthier and Moonhunter were from Ch'bauldi dragons, they might seek to control the special living being germinating within the orb. And that was why the orb held great value, and my failure at keeping it safe was so severe.

"It is an oracle's orb and contains enlightened stardust." It was accurate enough and certainly enough to appease their questions for now, I hoped.

"An oracle's enlightened globe?" Balthier asked slowly, annunciating every word with emphasis. His eyes held an amused twinkle. "Then why was it glued to the hand of a poor broken monk statue?"

He did have a point. I couldn't help my shrug. "I suspect it was meant as a joke. Monks, ninjas... don't people think we're pretty much the same thing anyway?"

"Except you're a woman!" Moonhunter protested. "Monks are men."

Balthier made a disconcerted face. There would definitely be a discussion between him and his apprentice after this meeting. I thought that maybe I would follow in one of their shadows just to hear what was said. Sometimes, it's fun to be a fly on the wall. Instead, I just stared at Moonhunter as if I knew something that he didn't and after a moment he squirmed unpleasantly under my gaze. "Only men can be monks," I muttered disappointedly and shook my head. This, I followed with a very quick scoff just to further drive home my taunting displeasure.

Balthier shot Moonhunter another look before Moonhunter could say anything further and humiliate them both more. "So how do you think that we can help you to find whoever has taken this? Wouldn't you be better finding a Drifter who locates items, or possibly a watcher?" Balthier asked.

I was beginning to wonder if they had listened to a single word I had already told them. "What part of 'dangerous' did you not understand? There isn't a single Drifter or watcher who would accept this mission because of the risk. Yet I don't know where in the Wells the statue has been taken and what travel might be required. So, a novihomidrak is my most likely choice."

Balthier looked like he had pieced together a fraction of the puzzle. His eyes briefly went to Moonhunter, which told me that he had figured out that I had no need of a Drifter to trace the item because of Moonhunter's connection to it. Dang, he was good.

"So, will you accept my quest?" I asked. I raised my hand and uncurled my fingers from around my palm where I held two little golden balls within. I wasn't sure if the novihomidraks would recognize them or not, though I knew I could place odds on a guess that Balthier would.

He sneered. "Influence energy," he growled.

I nodded. "Certainly, but not intended for use on either of you. I would much rather have you doing this of your own free will. Rather, it is a down payment."

I extended my hand toward Balthier.

He didn't move forward to accept them. "How do we know that it's influence and not chaos that you have within them?"

"Until you use them, you only have my word. But even if it were chaos, might that not be helpful in certain circumstances, especially if you were a tight pinch?" I continued to keep my hand raised.

The look on Moonhunter's face told me that this was a whole new circumstance for him, and that he'd had no prior experience with anything of this caliber, but he also knew Balthier well enough to know that the stakes of this game had reached an extreme level. Clever boy.

"You'll need to part with some real money or something of worth to get the mission completed," Balthier said.

I felt the nerves hit my stomach as the bluff in my game had been called. I wondered just how much I would really have to pay. "Once the orb is returned, I will be able to fulfill your request."

Balthier smiled brutally. "Once you can show your face and address whatever you call your council of ninjas. Isn't that right?"

He knew. I wondered if his novihomidrak senses could hear the steady hammering of my heart. What more of an answer did he need than that? His brown eyes never flinched from mine. He knew that if I admitted that I'd lost the orb, the Black Nights would slaughter me and trap my energy for all of eternity. What the ninjas could do to any other energy paled in comparison to what they could inflict upon another Black Night.

"You will have your money," I promised.

Balthier lifted the two golden balls of influence energy from my palm. "Then I shall make sure to hold onto one of these in case I need to persuade you further when the time comes."

If that was what the novihomidrak wanted to believe, there wasn't much I could do to convince him otherwise. "I must now leave this adventure in your capable hands," I said as I bowed my head toward them.

"Does that mean you're not going to be hanging around?" Balthier asked.

I tried really hard not to smile. Some say that when a soul-colist smiles, it is the most chilling thing anyone living has ever seen. Being a ninja, I had mastered it. "I have other details to which I must see to right now." Those aspects involved being in the shadows, trying to feel along the energy that the novihomidraks were going to go, and easing their path so that no one could interfere with them. I figured Balthier already knew this was my plan and there was no need to scare the boy. I would let him take my words at face value and let him think that I had other business to attend. But the truth was that only his energy was capable of finding the stardust monk. I would be following it very carefully.

Balthier nodded.

"Then it is settled," the Grand Sapere said. He tried really hard not to flinch when he looked at me, but he did. I knew he was anxious to have me out of his sanctuary.

"As I am here, Grand Sapere, would you like me to go around and make a soul collection before I go?" I said it just to make the Grand Sapere nervous. Again, I had to control myself to keep from smiling.

A flash of heat went through him and soon he'd break out in sweat. "That really won't be necessary," he said rather hurriedly.

I bowed my head, but this time in the direction of the Grand Sapere. "Then I shall take my leave." I turned and walked from the room going through the doorway before I let myself evaporate into the shadowplane along the wall. I had to let them see me leave the room first, or they would think that I hadn't left. Not that I couldn't now shadowwalk back inside, but at the moment I was probably better off waiting. With the noviho-midraks aware of my presence, they might feel me re-enter. I still wasn't sure this would fool Balthier. He probably already suspected that I would be waiting for them, but I doubted he would raise a fuss at this point. He knew just how much I needed them, both to travel with and to find the stardust monk.

I heard their muffled voices from inside the room. It didn't sound like arguing, but rather just finalizing this mission. The worst thing that the Grand Sapere said was to keep me from returning to his temple at all costs. Balthier grunted in agreement.

After another quick, muted discussion, Balthier came first out into the hallway, followed shortly by Moonhunter.

"So what's –" Moonhunter began, but Balthier interrupted him by raising a hand. Balthier looked around, his eyes covered with the red dragon lids.

"Say nothing," Balthier warned. "I can't see her, but that doesn't mean she's not around."

Moonhunter took Balthier's lead by blinking down his dragon lids too and began to follow behind Balthier. They headed to the room that the saperes had set up for their novi-homidrak guests. Balthier closed the door behind him and Moonhunter, but could not lock it. Apparently, the saperes figured the novihomidraks didn't have to be worried about being locked in to guard against outside intrusion. Moon-hunter crossed the room, still looking at everything as he went. Standing in front of the window, he turned and blinked back the lids. He waited for Balthier to finish sweeping the room with his gaze as well.

Moonhunter made to speak. Once again, Balthier lifted his hand and hushed Moonhunter.

"Ninjas work with energy. I know she's in the room with us, but even though we cannot see her or feel her, it doesn't mean that she's not here."

Balthier's words left confusion on Moonhunter's face. He definitely had no experience with ninjas. "She purchased us for this quest. If we can't discuss it because we are afraid she is around, how will we get this case done?" Moonhunter asked.

The boy's logic was astonishing. Balthier's face reddened with anger, knowing that Moonhunter had a point.

Balthier pulled out a chair from the desk and dragged it over to the polished dark wood table sitting closer to the window. He also grabbed up a piece of paper and a pen, then seated himself to begin to make notes. "Okay, we'll handle is just like any other case then, if you insist. I guarantee you though; this is going to get us burned."

Moonhunter turned slightly so Balthier couldn't see him rolling his eyes. He straightened and returned to being casual. "So what do we know?"

"We know that there's an ugly and chipped monk statue missing out there somewhere and we're assigned to look for the damned thing. Who would ever want that god-awful thing, I don't know. But, the orb on it is special." Balthier scratched away at the papers as he began to make notes about the things he was saying. He certainly did not seem pleased. "Apparently, that orb contained stardust, or something else, which seems to be from your origin home world. We have no evidence, only that it appears that way." Balthier scratched three lines under the words *seemed to be* as if emphasizing them now and forever.

"If it's not stardust in the orb, what else could it be?"

"Let us hope it is only stardust. Anything more could be extremely dangerous."

Moonhunter came to stand closer to the table so he could read the notes that Balthier was making. "So why do you think I'm so drawn to it? Other than it's from my home world. There's got to be something else, right?"

Balthier raised the pen into the air, his hand twitching a couple times as if he were tapping it against something. "The Humline has been telling me that as well. I think we should explore that. I do have a theory, though it sounds quite wild and outlandish."

"What?" Moonhunter asked eagerly.

Balthier glanced around the room again, searching. Then he returned his gaze to Moonhunter and set down the pen. In that moment of silent communication, Balthier made his decision. He rose from his chair and stepped away from the table.

Once he had some room around him, he raised his arms and made broad sweeping circles around him. Energy crackled fiercely in the air and the novihomidrak's magic had a sharp sting in it. Around Balthier appeared a magnificent web of flowing lines, glowing points, and multicolored threads moving in every direction. Balthier gestured for his apprentice to approach. Moonhunter walked right through the web which parted and then healed right behind him.

Balthier reached up and pulled on a gold thread wrapped with red. As soon as he did, much of the webbing dissolved away from the strand hooked on his finger, Balthier flicked the fingers of his other hand and more of the netting fell away. "This is actually a piece of the past, a memory that Vehlka gave me when she called for me to attend your birthing." Balthier looked at Moonhunter as if trying to send him the meaning of something deeper in his words. "Hold on to this for a moment."

Moonhunter reached out, circled the thread over his finger, and held it while Balthier went searching backwards along the thread. Moonhunter craned his neck in order to watch Balthier. His features softened and after a moment, Balthier looked up sharply and made a tutting sound at

Moonhunter. "No prying into your dragon mother's life," Balthier warned fiercely.

"Sorry. I just wanted to see if I could get a sense of her."

Balthier reached up and snagged a thread very close to the gold entwined thread that he gripped. He held it out toward Moonhunter. "I should have known that by this stage of your development, you would be getting curious about your novimather. This'll give you a small glimpse of who she was, of how I knew her."

Careful to keep his hold onto the thread he held, Moonhunter twisted and had to spin around in order to accept the thread that Balthier offered in the other hand. Again, his face softened as his eyes mostly closed. He chuckled. That seemed to please Balthier, who also smiled and gave a murmur of his own.

"Do you think this has to do with my dragon mother then?" Moonhunter asked.

"Now just hold on," Balthier scolded. "Give me a moment to look."

Moonhunter released the thread he had a hold of and it slowly drifted back to its original position. He tried to patiently wait for Balthier, but his foot kept twitching as if he wanted to tap it. After a moment, he started looking around, then turned his back to Balthier and started blinking his eyes. He made the dragon lids go down, then up, then down, then up. After doing in this in rapid succession about twenty times or so, he added in snarling with his dragon teeth every six blinks for so.

"Moon," Balthier snapped impatiently.

Moonhunter jumped and spun around to face Balthier. "Yes?" he asked innocently.

Balthier suddenly broke into a large smile. "Is that blood I see? Are you playing with your teeth again?"

"I don't know what you're talking about," Moonhunter

said rapidly as he dragged his arm across his mouth and sucked in tight on his lips in order to vacuum all of the blood and spit out of it.

"When you decide to grow a pair of fangs, let me know. Until then, quit playing with your baby teeth," Balthier teased. "You can let go of the thread now. Come over here. I want to show you this."

The novihomidraks huddled very close to a little sparkling spot on the golden thread. "It's like a gem," Moonhunter remarked.

"That it is." Balthier reached out with his finger and whispered something. The scent of novihomidrak magic once again brightened in the air. The little twinkle rolled onto Balthier's fingernail. He let go of the thread and turned toward Moonhunter. "Here," he said taking a light hold on Moonhunter's chin. Moonhunter's eyes carefully followed the little glint on Balthier's fingernail as Balthier brought it toward his temple. When he lost sight of it in his peripheral vision, his face twitched, but Balthier had a hold of him and Moonhunter's head did not turn. Balthier let the sparkle roll from his fingertip onto Moonhunter's temple. The twinkle lingered there for a moment then vanished. Moonhunter's eyes widened as a look of surprised excitement came over his face. "You think my mother is responsible for this?"

"It would seem to be. And, it would make sense."

"But if it's true..."

"I don't think Vehlka would go that far, so speak no more of it."

Balthier dismissed the dazzling web from the room and went back to the table. He sat back down and took up the pen again only to tap it against the pad of paper.

I hoped he would write something and when he didn't I really wanted to step from the shadows and yell at them until he told me what he knew. I had to control my energy. This was too important to mess it up now.

"So, Moonhunter, where do we start to look?"

"I don't know," Moonhunter answered. "Do you think a subprog would help us?"

Balthier had the look of a mentor who was pleased that his student was progressing. He nodded. "I think a subliminal programmed question is exactly what we need. Besides that, you need practice at it anyway." Even though Balthier had made that last line sound sharp, he most likely hadn't meant it as anything other than a jest.

"Then I shall return to our ship now and get what we need for the subprog." Moonhunter bowed to Balthier, then headed for the door. "Then, after that, can we please go get something to eat?"

"What? And miss whatever meal the fine saperes have prepared for us?"

"Please!"

"I'll think about it." Balthier waited until Moonhunter was out of the room before he started to laugh and shook his head. "My apprentice sure does amuse me sometimes."

Balthier kicked back in his chair and picked up the notes to review them. The room fell silent. After a moment, Balthier continued, "I would be most displeased if something happened to my apprentice. Come out of the shadows and let's you and I have a discussion."

I debated for another moment whether I should fulfill Balthier's request or not. Did he really know that I was there, or was he just making a haphazard guess? What did it matter if he threatened an empty room. There was no embarrassment for yelling at the shadows if he was truly alone. But I was curious as to what other information he thought I might be able to provide, so I obliged.

"I knew you were there," Balthier growled. He tossed the

notes down on the table, the cardboard backing of the pad of paper making a thump on the wood.

"I didn't know novihomidraks made notes," I said. "I thought your memories retained everything."

"It does. I recall the details of many missions. But I like the act of taking notes," Balthier explained, though he sounded kind of testy that he found himself doing such a thing. "I find that it slows down my thoughts and clears my head, filtering everything down to only that which is important."

I reached out to the pad of paper and turned it with just my fingertips. "And you think this is the relevant information?"

"I think I'll definitely need to pick up a case of Telxean wine before we head out. I'll need something to dull my senses, so that I'm not always actively looking in the shadows." Balthier kicked back putting one foot up on the table, then crossing the other on top of it.

I recognized the sharp jab, yet another one meant for me. "You know how it must be, how I must travel. I very much doubt that you would make an offer to make this easier on me, so I will resort to whatever needs I must take in order to be there with you and Moonhunter."

Balthier reached down and twisted a thick ring which enwrapped his finger. It held a rather large oval stone of the gaudiest gray and blue I had ever seen, but his energy was so tightly wound with it that I knew I had found the novihomidrak's sacred object. In realizing that I had seen it, he dropped feet off the table and sank his hand down to his side as if he could hide the ring behind his leg. Novihomidraks did not like giving up their secrets.

"So, you have worries about your apprentice," I said, harvesting his words to bring our conversation back to the reason I had come out of the shadows. "Let us discuss."

"The way I figure it, since you were guarding the thing, you've got to know way more about who took it than what you have said so far." Balthier leaned back, casually crossing one leg over his knee, and looking perfectly at ease, but I knew better than that. Novihomidraks did not relax easily, especially in the presence of a soulcolist ninja. Certainly not one who now knew the sacred object.

I held out my hands and allowed the willing molecules in the air to slow and solidify into the shape of a chair. I took a seat as well. This allowed me to be on the same level as Balthier without having to look down upon him. I thought meeting him at his eye level might be a better way to befriend him rather than to keep up this coarseness between us. I certainly did not want him believing that he was subservient to me and that was how it felt with me standing over him. "I realize our time is short as Moonhunter is already reaching the ship. My name is Calliesar, and I am originally from the Belex galaxy. I served for fifty years in my system as a soulcolist before becoming a ninja, for which I have served another thirty years in that capacity. I have been guardian of the orb for nearly twenty-five, so you must understand that this is not a regular thieving. This has been planned. And I suspect someone from the Dragon Council is in on it. If the orb were to get into the wrong hands, it could be very devastating."

"Why would the Dragon Council want an orb of stardust?"

"It is as you suspect," I admitted, holding my hands together. "This is Vehlka's special birth."

Balthier tried to keep the righteously smug look off of his face, but he didn't quite succeed. He exaggerated his shock and failed at that as well. Of course, for a novihomidrak of Balthier's age who had seen many worlds in the Wells, he probably had quite a list of accomplishments. Fortunately, acting was not a skill he had ever acquired.

"So, has Moonhunter been selected as Guardian of her special birth?" Balthier asked and I did not mock him for the worried tone in his voice. He had every right for concern. "Is that why he is so drawn to the orb?"

"No, your apprentice will still be your own. We both know that he is not ready to take a guardianship position."

"Well, certainly it is not me." Fear shown in his eyes. "I have no feelings toward the orb whatsoever."

"My first concern is getting the orb back. My second concern will be keeping it out of the hands of the Dragon Council. I believe it is with Moonhunter's connection through the Humline of his home galaxy, that we shall find the right course of action for the orb."

"So if you think the Dragon Council is in on this, why are you hiring novihomidraks?" Balthier asked.

"Because, chances are that it was a novihomidrak who originally stole it."

Hackles seemed to rise along Balthier's neck. Somehow, I knew that little bit of knowledge would get under his skin. Especially now that he had figured out that his own dragon mother was involved. Now, this became personal.

"And you think that novihomidrak is not its new Guardian?"

"No, I don't believe it is."

Balthier's gaze shifted toward the door. "If you're going to stay for the subprog, I suggest you get back in the shadows now."

I felt a little surprised that Balthier would actually offer to let me stay for the novihomidrak ritual. I merely nodded, then stepped to the side. Back into the shadows I disbursed.

A moment later, the door opened and Moonhunter entered. He carried with him a small black leather bag which looked rather lumpy. He brought it over to the table and set it down on top by Balthier's notes. "Did you already go get a sapere or shall I?" Moonhunter asked.

Balthier's mouth puckered into a frown. "I think we shall try this without a sapere. I have a feeling this could be very sensitive and I don't trust any of the saperes here and what they would report to the Dragon Council."

"Really?" Moonhunter put his hand on the black bag and slid it toward him just a little bit. "But isn't that risky?"

"Anything dealing with a sapere is risky," Balthier said sarcastically. "You would do well to learn that before your friends graduate from the temple. Trusting them too much at some point might cost you your life. Just because they are favored by Ch'bauldi dragons and have pledged their loyalty to them, does not mean they will remain loyal to you."

Moonhunter looked visibly shaken. His energies got all chaotic with questions and the restraint that it took to hold them back. His curiosity was intense, but his self-preservation stronger.

Balthier seemed embarrassed by all he had just said. He shook his head and rubbed his hand fiercely against his forehead. "I probably have said too much. I just want you to be aware of all the things that can happen to a novihomidrak. For as invincible as we wish to seem, that is not always the case. We deal with a lot of things, and sometimes the conspiracies that we fight come from within. We can't always pick our struggles, but it is important that we survive through them."

Moonhunter nodded his agreement. "I understand."

"You are young and just beginning. When you are as old as I am, and have seen the things that I have seen, then you will see why I am always so harsh. I suspect that this mission will certainly bring you a new depth of understanding, one I wish I didn't have to give you, but a lesson that may be best learned now rather than when you are out on your own."

The boy seemed genuinely scared now, and maybe he should be.

"Shall we be to this?" Balthier asked.

Moonhunter looked at the new chair that had been added to the room and sat down. "I trust you, Balthier," he said. "Let's do this."

Balthier unzipped the bag and began setting a variety of items on the table: a feather quill pen, a crystal, a crystal ball, a book, and a little bell. He took the empty bag and tossed it onto the bed. As he circled around Moonhunter, Balthier waved his hands around the boy. He never touched Moonhunter, but it looked like he was pulling something off of him. With the shift, I felt the chaos energy fall away. Balthier was cleaning Moonhunter of all negativity. Whether or not they wanted to admit it, they worked with just as much energy as anyone else.

"Close your eyes and relax," Balthier instructed. As Moonhunter's eyes closed, he let his shoulders relax down.

"I want you to focus on the statue. Think about the first time you saw it," Balthier said, giving a little snicker, "since the second time you saw it you were more concerned with saving it." That brought a little smile to Moonhunter's lips as well.

Balthier walked around Moonhunter again and a protective circle went up around the boy. Balthier extended the circle to encompass the table, which he had to drag away slightly from the wall in order to walk behind it. It seemed like the table even shrunk just a little bit for him. Balthier lowered his dragon lids and searched along the outer rim of each circle. He picked away a couple strands that still clung to it. With a clap of his hands, a thick golden candle appeared on the table already lit. The light from the candle made the edges of the magical circles glow with red and gold.

"Tell me about the statue. What do you see?" Balthier asked. He quickly flipped open the book, its pages empty. He took the feather quill and stood it up over the page.

"It's in the garden at that bed-and-breakfast that we stayed at," Moonhunter said. "I loved to look at it each morning in the sunlight. The orb would change colors as the sun rose. It's almost like it was praising its fellow star for greeting the day. It felt like a song and even though I was watching it, it seemed more like an emotion I was hearing."

As Moonhunter spoke, the page of the book filled with not only words from Moonhunter, but images as well. The pen scratched quickly, hurrying to get it all down. A small stream of light came from the center of Moonhunter's forehead and flowed to the feathered end of the quill.

"How does it make you feel?"

"I don't know exactly. Part of me wants to pick up the statue and run away with it. There's something in the Humline, I can feel it, but I can't identify it. I'm a little afraid that I'll never see it again. No, I'm a lot afraid I won't see it again. I have to take it. I know my master won't be happy if I steal it. I have to leave here. The Humline knows that it's almost time. They're coming for it. They're coming for it!" His voice grew panicked the more he spoke.

Balthier leaned closer to Moonhunter and quickly whispered something in the novihomidrak language. "Moonhunter," he said, standing upright once again, "stay with it. Follow that thought. I pinned it."

Moonhunter nodded his head. He placed his hands to rest on his lap though his fingers now curled and uncurled against his thighs. His foot tapped.

"Moon, relax," Balthier ordered.

Moonhunter gave a shake that went through his a head

and shoulders while he took a deep breath. Trying to relax only seemed to be making him more nervous.

"You said they were coming to get the statue and you knew that they were coming. Who are they?"

"I don't know. I just feel them coming. My only chance is if I escape with Moonhunter. He's going to take me to her."

"Her?" Balthier asked as he looked around, clearly searching the shadows. "Where is Moonhunter supposed to take you?"

A motion jerked through Moonhunter's leg, partially lifting his knee and twisting his leg as though he wanted to walk. He twitched, almost a spasm. "To her. But it's too early; she's still a baby. I have to wait."

Concern flickered across Balthier's face. "Your name is Moonhunter. You are not the statue. Moonhunter, follow the thread along the Humline. Who is coming? Follow it, go to that point where someone other than you will pick it up."

Moonhunter nodded again. "The statue is being sold. The guy is a collector, or so he says. The Humline is telling me his words aren't true. Or not entirely accurate. He knows what this is. He wants it. He wants to control the dragon. He knows a new species is being born." Moonhunter doubled over and covered his face with his hands. He cried out as if it hurt him. His talons extended and he grabbed at his black hair and pulled. Balthier rushed forward and tried to break Moonhunter's grip. Moonhunter screamed.

"Mezzipalor nak'ta shae."

At Balthier's words, Moonhunter slumped down in his chair, his arms falling away from his head. Once more, he seemed totally relaxed. His eyes were open, but looked flat as if he saw nothing in the room around them.

Balthier, on the other hand, was another story. He had begun to sweat. The channel of novihomidrak magic that he was pulling through himself was more than he was normally used to. Black masses of chaos energy were beginning to cling to the shell that surrounded them.

Balthier leaned forward over his knees and whispered once again to Moonhunter. He stood there for a while, half crouched, his hands on his knees while he panted heavily. He brought his hand up and made a swooping gesture in the air.

Atop the book, the quill continued to scratch away.

Tiredly, Bathier went to study the book for a moment. "Moonhunter, we were on a mission for the high vizier of the Dragon Council. Was this the man who took the statue? Was the vizier the one who took possession of the statue from the garden?"

"Yes."

Balthier leaned in again and whispered for a third time. Then, having recovered enough, he stood straight up once more. "Then what happened?"

Moonhunter sat silent for quite a significant amount of time. At first, Balthier stood there with Moonhunter, but then noticed the bits of chaos worming their way through the magical wall. As he waited, he went over and tried to brush away the negative energy. One piece he pushed off slammed right back into the wall so hard that it made Balthier jump.

The quill came to a stop.

Balthier turned back toward Moonhunter with a worried look. The feathered quill swayed. "Moonhunter, are you still with me?"

Moonhunter still did not speak. Balthier stepped in front of Moonhunter and bent down to look at the relaxed features of Moonhunter's face. After a moment, Balthier put a hand beneath the boy's chin and tipped back Moonhunter's head. "What happened to the statue after you were shot?"

Silence.

"What happened right before it was removed from its pedestal?"

It seemed as if Moonhunter was asleep, rather than sitting there in the chair. The quill began to move. Balthier leaned over to read what the quill was issuing.

Suddenly, all the magic dropped. Balthier turned in a full circle, his eyes red from the dragon lids. "Calliesar, go get a sapere, now!"

I felt my own energy scatter as Moonhunter pitched forward into Balthier's arms. All would be lost if something happened to Moonhunter. I composed myself and slid from the shadows as Balthier lowered Moonhunter to the ground. I hesitated and my pause received a narrowed glare from Balthier; he certainly didn't like repeating himself. I stepped sideways, more as a habit of my usual movements, then reached for the door and ran out into the hallway. Was I to grab the first sapere I saw, or did I need to fetch the Grand Sapere? I realized that I didn't know enough about what the novihomidraks were up to in order to understand how to help. I thought about returning to ask Balthier, but I didn't want to face his wrath. I'd watched him long enough to know that he didn't suffer fools, which he would certainly consider me one now.

I ran down the halls looking for a sapere.

Why could one never be found when one was needed?

I turned, not sure where I was going, only that I needed to be hurrying. Still, no saperes.

I felt for energy throughout the building, something, anything. It seemed like absolutely nothing surrounded me. That, as I well knew, was impossible.

I had lost myself.

No, my energy had been tethered with Moonhunter's, and it was his that was lost.

What exactly had happened? I didn't understand enough of this.

"Ninja," I heard a voice call from down the hallway behind me. I turned at the sound. "Ninja," it repeated.

"Where are you?" I yelled back.

"You're no ninja, are you?" the voice teased. "You're old and pathetic. You've lost your abilities. Once you were great and powerful, but now you are rigid and declining."

"Now you've made me mad," I shouted, storming down the hall with tight fists at my sides ready to punch something.

"Oh are you now? I'm so scared."

"Don't taunt me. Just show me where you are. Give me back Moonhunter."

The walls seemed to shift. I felt the rippling in the energy as if it were a kaleidoscope being turned.

"How will you feel, Calliesar, to know that you been involved in trapping a novihomidrak within his own subconsciousness?" the voice called out. "Will you have any remorse at all?"

Now that the words had been spoken, I knew what was going on: my energy had been trapped. But who had done it? Balthier? He seemed a likely suspect. He had to know that his days as a novihomidrak were coming to an end. To what lengths would that drive him, especially if he had a chance to secure his future? A cushy seat on the Dragon Council maybe? Could it be Moonhunter leading me into an ambush? Highly unlikely, but still a possibility. Being a naïve young boy might just be part of his act. Balthier may have made him very cunning. Or, could it be the novihomidrak that currently possessed this monk statue with the orb? Even as I pondered these possibilities, I stretched out for whatever energy was around trying to contain me. I swore that the novihomidrak responsible for this would pay dearly as only a soulcolist could make a novihomidrak do.

I raised a hand and merely thought about cutting a doorway out of here as my fingers made the swipes to form the doorway. Bright black lines ripped into the surroundings. I pushed the door forward and it dropped away like a falling plank. I found myself once more in the hallway of the real temple. The influx of energy caught me slightly off guard. I hadn't remembered there being quite so many saperes here, but I also had to account for the energy of two novihomidraks.

I hurried down the real hallway and came across a girl who looked like she might be an acolyte. She looked half scared to see me as I reached out for her. She stepped back away from my touch. "I need a sapere capable of working higher magicks in conjunction with a novihomidrak's power," I said hurriedly. "Find me one now."

The girl shrank back, a little more in terror, but nodded her head in understanding. Then she turned around and ran down the hall.

I, meanwhile, turned around and went back to the spot where I had cut the door through the energy. The flat rectangular slab still lay on the floor. The chamber beyond, meant to contain my energy, was also still there. I removed a bracelet of black bone from my wrist and held it up. Looking through the center of the bracelet I could see the webbing energy that composed this structure of non-reality. But would it hold the secrets of who had made it? This tight weave definitely indicated novihomidrak magic. It had absolutely been meant for a prison, but intended for someone much weaker, someone not capable of breaking out. And when I discovered that fact within the workings of the magic, I understood that it hadn't been meant to contain me for very long, but rather as a way to distract me. But divert me from what?

Moonhunter.

He held the key to all this. Without him, we might not ever be able to track the monk statue.

I lay my hand upon the spell and drew in all of its energy.

The hardy strength made my head whirl for a moment. When I was done, I rotated my hand. A little golden ball which held all of the energy from the spell appeared in my palm. I dropped it in my pocket, knowing that I would have time later to study it, to decipher whose magic it was. But now, Moonhunter took precedence.

With the spell out of the way, I hurried back down the hall to the novihomidrak's room. Balthier had lifted Moonhunter from the floor and taken him over to the bed. Balthier looked up at me as I entered. "Is a sapere on the way?" he asked.

"An acolyte is fetching one." I stepped over to the bed and looked down at Moonhunter's pale countenance. "What happened and how can a sapere help?" I asked.

As I stood there feeling a little helpless, Balthier pretended to ignore me.

"Maybe there is something I can do to help. Whatever trapped Moonhunter also tried to trap me." I knew I was laying a lot out on the table by telling Balthier. He could very well be the one responsible for this. But I had to trust that his concern for his apprentice was real. I had never seen a novihomidrak master treat their apprentice so kindly, not that I had seen many, but enough to make me feel like this was an extraordinary circumstance between the two of them and that they had a strong relationship built.

"Define what you mean by that," Balthier said.

"When I left to get a sapere, someone trapped me inside an energy prison. Not a strong one. Obviously they'd been hoping for someone else."

"I take it you captured what you could."

I nodded. "I did."

"So will you be able to trace the energy?" Balthier asked.

"With time," I responded. Frustration was starting to creep into my tone no matter how I tried to hold it back.

Time was not a thing I felt we had a lot of, but Balthier wouldn't quit asking his questions.

Balthier looked down at Moonhunter, then back at me. He glanced to the door, anguish clearly played on his face. "I'm afraid a sapere won't make it before he's pulled under. Is there anything you can do to help?" Fingers curled into fists. "I should've never tried to do this without a sapere."

I knelt down beside the bed, laced my fingers together, and stretched my arms. "You did that because I suggested the Dragon Council might be involved. You were just doing what you thought was best, what you thought would safeguard Moonhunter." I dug in my pocket and took out the little ball, then handed it to Balthier. "This is the energy I collected. If I fail, find another ninja who can interpret that energy for you. If nothing else, it will point you at a target."

Balthier took the ball from my fingers and glared at it sternly as if he could right the situation with just a look.

I turned over Moonhunter's hand and placed my middle finger into the center of his palm. Then I reached up and placed the middle finger of my other hand over the top of his heart. I took steadying breaths, the first two for me, then the rest to fall into rhythm with Moonhunter's breathing. I felt our hearts begin to match pace. It only took a moment to find and secure his energy.

Balthier shifted nervously, and I knew he had good reason. If he knew anything about me and my practices, then he knew that this was the way for a soulcolist to gently take a life and extract the energy of the person. But I had no need to extract Moonhunter's energy or his experiences, not at this moment at least. I needed him very much alive, and I hoped that Balthier understood enough so that he would not interrupt the performance.

To do this, I had to match Moonhunter's energy. It

required me to put myself in such a state that I no longer had conscious awareness of myself but only him.

I had a sudden perception of Moonhunter when he'd been undergoing the spell, how he had believed that he was the orb. He had done exactly what I was attempting to do now. A part of me knew that with all things being connected, I could actually touch the orb's energy now through Moonhunter. Could I locate it without him? As certain as I was that the novihomidraks would be glad to get rid of me, I also realized what I was potentially going up against: another novihomidrak. Unfortunately, it still remained safer for me to keep Balthier and Moonhunter at my side as we located the item. But, if in doing this, I had the opportunity to discover the orb, I would do it.

It would help us all in the long run, especially if I could figure out who possessed the orb right now. That would simplify things immensely. Because while we took the time to travel for the orb, we could also research everything about the person holding it. We could go in with a plan of attack instead of being blind. My mind made up to go through with this, I attuned my energy into Moonhunter's. I appeared beside a well, not one of the Wells that the dragons used to travel through, but an actual water well. A boy sat on the stone ledge. He resembled a younger, much more darling Moonhunter.

He had a headful of much tighter curls than his teenage-self did. Short, round legs swung in the air and he knocked his heels playfully against the rock. Even though I could smell a forest of trees and just a hint of smoke, everything else around us was white.

I approached slowly, cautiously. I knew that this might just be an image that Moonhunter's mind had created as a form of the Wells to which he was so used to traveling. If the little boy version of him tried to go through it, would I even be able to follow? Would I find him again? It might just drive him deeper into his subconscious.

The boy turned around and began to dangle his fingers over the edge of the well. He giggled.

"What's down there?" I asked, curiosity nearly overcoming precaution.

"My mother," the boy replied enthusiastically. "Not my real mother, but my dragon mother and all of her other little babies. Do you want to see?"

As I drew closer, I realized why his dragon mother had been so entranced with this little boy, enough to take him and carry him with her for the next ten years while he became a novihomidrak. Time aged everyone's aura and changed their colors depending on their life progression. The joy and innocence within Moonhunter's young aura was so clean that it was nearly clear, like looking through unpolluted air toward the clarity of a flawless blue sky. That's how it felt to look at him. I came up beside the well, still afraid that he might jump, but the fear not nearly as overwhelming while being in his presence. He had such a calming attitude about him.

His fingers dipped in the water. I had never seen a well with the water level so high. Something very large had to be down there in order to displace the water so much.

Moonhunter laughed as a squiggly gold line came up and nibbled at his fingers. "Did you see it? That was one of her babies."

So Moonhunter's dragon mother had just given birth right before taking Moonhunter and he had seen them as a little boy. No wonder he was so connected to her special birth. I wondered if she had planned it that way.

"I did."

Several more red and gold lines squiggled their way up to nudge against Moonhunter's fingers. "They can't actually hurt me, you know? I'm protected by my dragon mother's shell."

"Yes, Moonhunter, you are indeed a very special little boy."

He tossed his beautiful brown curls as he beamed up at her with the brightest of smiles. "I'm going to be a great novihomidrak someday," he announced proudly.

"I have no doubt about that." I reached my hand out toward the boy, but did not touch him. For this, he had to be very willing. "We need to get going back now, Moonhunter. It's time you know?"

Moonhunter transformed into the older novihomidrak that he was. "I'm glad you came and got me."

"I don't think either one of you will be going anywhere anytime soon." The voice started out coming from all around them but then coalesced to point right behind them.

I whirled around and set Moonhunter behind me. As soon as I saw the black and silver cloak, I wished I'd put Moonhunter in front of me. I knew I'd been right in asking for the help of two novihomidraks up against another novihomidrak. But now I knew a deeper truth: my novihomidrak nemesis had dabbled in the dark magicks. He was a Necronosti.

The Necronosti raised his head enough that I could see the man smiling. Or, I'd suspected it to be a man, until I noticed it was actually a woman.

"You must be pretty crazy to be a female novihomidrak dabbling in the darker magicks," I stated, trying not to show my fear.

The woman lowered her hood, showing off a magnificent green dragon tattoo circling her left eye from her forehead to her cheek. It matched the emerald of her eyes and looked stunning with her blonde hair. She looked almost like she could be an elven queen. "Everyone has their price."

Moonhunter came around me, his dragon teeth extended and his talons out. "Pathetic green dragon slime! Your magic is puny compared to mine."

She laughed at Moonhunter. "You are a young Ch'bauldi novihomidrak. While your mother was ancient, you were her last born, and you no longer have the protection of her life. Dispatching of you will be like killing a fly." Her lips kept twitching and her tongue flickered oddly over her teeth. The woman had trouble containing her own dragon aspects while in the presence of Moonhunter.

I felt Moonhunter's energy rise as he made for an attack, and I grabbed him before he did so. I threw my arms around his chest in order to keep him with me. I was half afraid he'd attack me. "Do not challenge her," I said, working language magic around him. I had to influence him and fast.

Moonhunter growled and spit landed on my skin. But at least he did not charge into a further attack.

"Vochey," the Necronosti called out and a sword appeared in her left hand while a pistol appeared in her right.

I instantly regretted the fact that I had matched my energy to Moonhunter's. Had I not, I could stand between him and a bullet, and most likely survive by merely adjusting my energy. But since I had taken on his novihomidrak energy, I could also be killed by novihomidrak weapons. I had picked up the same flaws that they had.

The Necronosti jerked the end of the pistol. "Move away. It's just the young novihomidrak I'm after. I have no reason to kill an aged ninja."

"Vochey Tranquility." As Moonhunter raised his hands, he seemed to pull on an invisible bow and string. The bow appeared in his hands already drawn with a notched arrow. He released the arrow and it struck the Necronosti.

I turned to Moonhunter, who was already reaching for a second arrow, and threw my arms around him.

A shot was fired from the pistol.

With the vortex of energy, I whirled us back to the real world. I slammed back into the physical form of my body with enough force that I hit the floor and skidded across the carpeted room. The bed cracked beneath Moonhunter as his own energy re-entered his figure, several of its wooden slats breaking and hitting the floor.

Balthier rushed over, his dragon aspects showing. "Are you all right?" he asked around his mouthful of dragon teeth.

"Necronosti," I said fearing that she might follow us through.

"I know. I felt it on Moonhunter's wave. That, and he had his bow."

If the energy of the bow had come back with us, I hoped it hadn't been broken in the vortex. I tried to sit. My ribs ached and the flair of pain kept me on the floor.

"Blood," Balthier said. "Were you injured?"

"Obviously, though I didn't realize until just now." I tried to look down at my rib cage and could barely lift my head. "The Necronosti shot me."

The sapere finally decided to show up at that moment. "I heard you needed – what happened in here?"

"Go get a transport. The Black Night has been shot. We need to get her to a hospital." Balthier whirled around to look at the sapere.

I reached up and grasped Balthier's hand. "Hospital won't do. I was attuned to novihomidrak energy. You need to treat me like a novihomidrak." If I hadn't been in such pain, I would've resented him calling me a Black Night. Especially after the Necronosti attack. The reasons ninjas prefer to be called ninjas was because of the Necronosti. The word Necronosti meant black night, but they were nothing like what we did. When people started calling us ninjas, we felt much better about taking that title. Since then, only in an official capacity were we ever called Black Nights. Having now been shot by a Necronosti, the last thing I wanted people to think about was a Black Night.

"You can't take the surgery of a novihomidrak to fix this," Balthier said.

"We really have no other choice," I argued with Balthier.

Balthier looked back at Moonhunter. "Since you helped Moonhunter, what can I do to help you?"

The sapere looked totally conflicted about what to do. This had to be way outside his realm of understanding. Much like so many other species throughout the universe, only a few rare people had understandings of what soulcolists even did as energy workers. And only soulcolists who could manipulate energy beyond that of someone's death, could become a ninja. Lack of that understanding is what brought most people their fear.

"We'll need another room," Balthier said to the sapere.

"We'll take her next door," the sapere replied.

"How is Moonhunter?" I asked.

"He'll be fine," Balthier scoffed, as though I was silly for even asking about Moonhunter.

"Is he conscious yet? I just want to make sure I've got all the energy of his essence. I lost control of the vortex. I had to do it fast and I probably didn't realize that I had been struck by a bullet at that point, but I'm sure it had an effect."

"He'll be fine," Balthier repeated. "Worry about you right now. You're losing a lot of blood." Balthier slid his arms under me. "This is probably going to hurt."

I tried not to scream as Balthier picked me up off the floor. Bright stars in a curtain of blackness floated around the edges of my vision as I fought to not pass out.

Balthier carried me from this room out into the hallway, and into the other room where the sapere ushered him.

"What did she mean we will have to handle this like a novihomidrak injury?" the sapere asked.

"She was merged with Moonhunter's energy when it happened."

Balthier's answer didn't seem to suit the Sapere. "Why was she merged with Moonhunter's energy?"

Balthier set me roughly down on the bed, probably more so than he meant to because of his irritation with the sapere. "Why should I have to explain our actions to you?" Balthier stormed. "It should be enough that we have told you that it needs to be done. Now let's begin."

I had to wonder how much Balthier was covering his own anguish at knowing that he should've originally called the sapere in and was directing his anger at the sapere now. Balthier reached down and pushed me over. "I'm sorry, but the bullet went in your back. Whatever you need to do, you'll have to do it lying on your stomach. What do you need from me?" he asked.

I lifted my left hand up and toward him. "I'll need to attune my energy to yours," I told him. "You're going to have to hold your left hand against my right hand since I can't move it. Make sure that my left hand stays over your heart."

Balthier didn't quite want to touch me as he fumbled about trying to figure out how this was supposed to work. I had to grab his hand and help him as much as I could. I gritted my teeth against the pain, as it settled in to be my friend for a while.

"How will I know when you're ready?" Balthier asked.

I couldn't even figure out a response to the question; I had already adjusted to Balthier's heartbeat. My head began to feel floaty as though I'd been too long on a carousel spinning around and around. The scent of smoke surrounded me.

My skin felt harsh, as though it were an old, tanned leather hide. So, this is what it felt like to be a timeworn novihomidrak.

Blackness around the edges of my vision crept closer. I thought about the ring Balthier wore around his finger. Various images came to mind, but they were all blurred together and I couldn't make any sense out of the scenes. The energy, however, was so strong. He had been through a lot and seen a lot of death. Small wonder that he had a subtle fear of soulcolists.

I began to hear the dragon language being spoken above me. It flowed through me with a power like I've never experienced before. I comprehended now why novihomidraks enjoyed what they did so much and why saperes trained for years to assist the novihomidraks with honor.

I relaxed. At least, until I felt the sharp pain rip through me. Behind my closed eyelids I saw bright flashes of red and green and gold as if all the colors were fighting. They were so intense that I wanted to look away, but since it was going on in my vision there was no way to escape it.

"What the −?" I heard Balthier say.

"She's not strong enough," the sapere remarked. "She's not a novihomidrak. Her body can't take this."

I realized I had returned to my own self-awareness. I tried to shift my focus back to Balthier, but I found him just as he cut off. Whether he knew it or not, he had put up a wall between us and I couldn't break it down.

At some point, I lost consciousness.

I woke to find Moonhunter standing over me. He smiled as I blinked and tried to focus on him. "I'm glad to see you're awake," he said.

I tried to lift my head but the unbearable pain made me set it right back down again.

"It'll take you a while," Moonhunter said. "After you passed out and lost the connection, Balthier had the idea that because of your connection to me, they might be able to get the bullet out with my novihomidrak weapons. I was still unconscious at the time so all he had was Tranquility and the one arrow notched onto it. They had to use the arrow tip to pull the bullet out. They got it, but since you were no longer connected with the novihomidrak magic, it's going to leave a scar."

With the bullet out and stitches having begun the healing, I knew that my own abilities could facilitate my recovery now. "There's something I might be able to do." I tried to sit up. "Just help me to my feet."

"I really don't think it's a good idea for you to move."

"I'll be fine now. I just need to stand so I can manipulate my own energy and get this all healed. We can't afford for me to be injured now."

As Moonhunter helped me rise up to my feet, I realized that I was no longer in the saperes' temple, nor was I in a hospital. I began to hear the steady hum of the engines of the spacecraft. I was on Balthier's ship.

"Here will be fine," I said, releasing my hold on Moonhunter. The accustomed black curtain filled with stars around the edges of my vision once more tried to draw across me and shut me off from the world. I resisted. "This may take some time." Then, I became a shadow.

Every molecule scattered.

Moonhunter glanced around, slapped his hands against his thighs, then he went to a chair that sat against the wall and dropped down into it to wait.

Dark matter swirled, pressing in every space not occupied by regular matter, in-between the tiny cracks and filling it in.

The energy felt so smooth.

The flight of the ship through space barely caused a ripple.

Before I could be lost in the moment, I gathered myself again and placed myself in the same room as Moonhunter. I stepped back out of the shadows and re-materialized. Moonhunter rose from his chair, ready to catch me just in case I fell. I didn't, but I appreciated his effort nevertheless.

"Are you all right?" Moonhunter asked, his arms still out and at the ready.

I shook my head, flinging off the weightlessness of comfort I felt in being my shadow-self. I checked my energy first, then physically reached back to where I'd been wounded. The area was tender, but no longer filled with unbearable pain. "Everything is all mended," I told him.

Moonhunter stared at me in disbelief. "How did you heal yourself so fast?"

"The body is nothing but a mass of energy. Everything within it knows its correct alignment. Soulcolists can easily realign their energy, being a ninja makes it easier."

"The dematerialization?"

Dematerialization. The ninjas called it shadow walking. But Moonhunter's word worked well enough, so I nodded.

"Where are we going?" I asked Moonhunter.

Moonhunter smiled and I was reminded of the little boy I'd seen by the well when he'd been so entranced by the baby dragons swimming around his fingers. I wanted to say something, but I knew that novihomidraks generally didn't recall their lives before their dragon mothers took them. Some said it was too dangerous for a novihomidrak to recall being swallowed by the dragon, that it would cause them to have a heart attack. I certainly didn't want to test the theory by accidentally making Moonhunter remember something he shouldn't. "We're heading to Klum in the Andieax system," he answered.

"Why are we going there?"

"Because you said that the novihomidrak was a female. There are very few females on the Dragon Council, and even fewer that are blonde. Balthier showed me their images and I pointed her out. She was stupid to lower her hood in front of us and even more so to let us get away. Now we know where she lives." His head tilted a little to the side. "Are you sure you're fully healed?"

My excitement jumped at the thought of nearly finding the statue with the orb. And yet, I knew that my time with it was coming to an end. "Yes, I am still a bit tired though," I said. It wasn't completely the truth.

"Then I'll let you get some rest," Moonhunter said kindly. "And I'll let Balthier know that you're awake."

"Very well." I started for the bed as Moonhunter went toward the door. Then I did something that ninjas rarely do, and usually only in extreme cases: I separated my energy from my body's essence. This, we called soul walking, and was extremely dangerous. As my body crawled into bed, my soul energy stepped into Moonhunter's shadow. I really hoped that he and Balthier would not sense me here. I worried for a moment when Moonhunter turned to look back into the room, but he was only giving my body one last glance to make sure that I was getting safely tucked in before he left. What a kind, kind boy.

Moonhunter crossed through the ship, and it appeared much vaster than expected. One would think that a noviho-midrak and his apprentice would have only a little two-person shuttlecraft, but this was significantly larger. For it to be run on a two-man crew seemed amazing. Unless Balthier hired more help, but he really didn't seem to be the type of person to do that. He seemed more likely to rely on only himself.

Moonhunter typed the combination into the keypad and the door to the flight deck opened. In here, it revealed that though the ship was big, it really had been designed for minimal crew. Balthier sat at the controls, neither hand on the rounded W-shaped flight control wheel before him. Instead, he held a palm-sized pad in one hand while he flipped through whatever he had on the tablet. Moonhunter didn't move close enough to see what Balthier was reading.

"I thought I'd let you know that Calliesar is awake."

"Good," Balthier grunted.

"What do you think is going to happen when we get to the planet?"

"Hopefully we find the orb as quickly as possible and get out of there with it," Balthier answered. "Strap in. We're landing soon."

As Moonhunter sat down and slid the harness over his chest, Balthier handed the tablet to him. It had a list of the Dragon Council members as well as their current living locations.

Balthier cleared them for landing and proceeded to the dock where he was instructed to go. The ship settled onto the surface of the planet.

"Should I go get Calliesar?" Moonhunter offered.

"No, not yet. Let's make sure there's no surprise waiting for us here." Balthier paused and gave a sour look to Moonhunter. "Magic dampeners. Do you feel them?"

Moonhunter nodded. "Strong ones too."

"With novies coming and going, I'm not surprised. It's probably the only way they can make sure we follow the rules."

Moonhunter cocked an eyebrow. "So, following the rules it is?"

"For the moment, I suppose."

It took several minutes before they were cleared to disembark. Upon opening the doors and lowering the ramp to leave, an official looking guy came striding out of the terminal across the tarmac toward them. He carried a clipboard by his side.

"I need your permission to search your ship," the man

demanded. He reached up and brushed back a straggly clump of wavy hair that fell over his eyes.

Balthier shrugged. "Why?"

"Landing procedures," he informed them. "It is our policy to search every ship that enters our port."

"Really? That must take an awful lot of manpower." Balthier looked around, easily seeing over a hundred ships already docked.

A line of sweat broke out on the man's forehead and made the curl that fell back down stick to his skin. "One can never be too cautious."

"And if I refuse to give you permission?" Balthier asked.

The man began to stammer. Obviously, he had not been prepped for this type of situation, or maybe he knew he was irritating a novihomidrak. Balthier stared at the man without even blinking. "But, it's policy," the man finally managed to blurt out.

"Since when?" Balthier growled. "Last night?"

The man swallowed, making his Adam's apple rise up and then fall. "If you don't sign this release for us to search your ship, I'll have to call security."

Balthier took the clipboard from the man's hands and began to read over the form clipped to it. He held it up, indicating that there was only one piece of paper on it. Balthier's eyes narrowed as he shook his head. "What kind of fools do you take us to be?"

"I don't understand."

"This society is advanced enough to be computerized. I'm surprised it's not on a tablet with a dainty little pen for me to sign. I also refuse to believe that you would have only one form on a clipboard. If you had wanted to make this look real, you would've photocopied about an extra fifteen of these or so. How old is this form? About twenty years old?" Balthier flipped the board around and pointed to a date at the bottom of the form. "Yeah, I expected you all to do a little bit better than that." Balthier shoved the board back in the man's chest. It actually made the man step backwards to catch himself before losing his balance.

As Balthier and Moonhunter tried to go around the man, he stepped back into their path and drew a pepper spray gun. He bit his tongue between his teeth as he gave a satisfied sneer.

Balthier, on the other hand, appeared unimpressed. Exhaling, his shoulders dropped down and he slid Moonhunter a here-we-go-again glance.

I stepped from where I had been standing in Moonhunter's shadow. The man looked at me in disbelief as I took to his shadow and dragged his energy out of him. I stepped into the man's body. "Wait!" I said, raising my hands quickly. "It's me, Calliesar. I've kicked him temporarily out of his body."

"Calliesar?" Balthier exclaimed.

"Yes, it's me," I said quickly, hoping to keep him from freaking out.

He looked the man over, while his lips twitched and his fingers curled. He struggled to control his dragon aspects.

"Get going, quickly!" I said to Moonhunter and Balthier, knowing I had to be quick to keep Balthier from asking where I had come from. I was fairly certain that he wouldn't like hearing that I had been hiding in Moonhunter's shadow. Especially considering how I'd surprised him.

Moonhunter stared at me in the man's body as he stepped around. "Is he dead?"

"No, not yet. I have about three minutes to release his energy. In that time, his energy will come springing back to him and it will seem like he just lost consciousness for a bit. Any longer than that though..." I let those words hang, the intention left unspoken. They understood what I meant.

"I had that handled," Balthier complained.

"Possibly, but my way is faster. Now, go. I've got to get back to my body. I'll meet you outside."

"Lock the door as you leave," Balthier said. "Five-six-two-thirty-seven is the code." He looked at Moonhunter and shrugged. "I didn't bother as we left."

"And you always yell at me about not locking up," Moonhunter teased.

They ran for the building that allowed them access to the docking port.

I stepped from the man's body and let him slump to the ground. Then I snapped the astral thread connecting my energy to my body and I boomeranged back to it with enough force that it rolled me right out of the bed and onto the floor. I jarred my wrist as I caught myself. I felt as if I had kissed the floorplates. At least I hadn't given myself a bloody nose. Standing, I popped my wrist and started for the exit. As I left the ship, I keyed in the numbers that Balthier had told me.

The man still lay unconscious on the tarmac, drool sliding out over his clipboard. I reached down and took the man's energy out once more in order to give myself a little more time. I followed the way I'd seen Balthier and Moonhunter travel.

Once inside, I had to slow my pace to not seem conspicuous. I felt the man's energy struggling in my hands. I probed it, trying to find answers to who had hired him. The energy refused to talk. With my silent interrogation going nowhere, I released the energy.

I rounded a corner and saw Moonhunter standing casually with his back to a wall, his arms crossed over his chest and one foot flat against the sheetrock. His eyes brightened when he saw me and for a moment, a thrill went through this old ninja. It tickled my fancy that someone could actually be waiting and excited to see me. It healed something deep inside my heart that I had nearly forgotten was there. Not that I had any illusions beyond that.

Moonhunter kicked away from the wall and matched my pace as we continued to hurry. Rounding another corner, I saw Balthier lower his tablet he'd been reading and rise from a chair where he'd been waiting. They had spaced themselves out in case I ran into trouble.

"We probably have another three minutes until he gains his senses enough to call for help," I told Balthier.

The older novihomidrak nodded with an acknowledging grunt. "Good. I've got an address."

We hurried out the entrance doors and Balthier called out for a helicab. I stepped back into Moonhunter's shadow.

"I really wish you wouldn't do that," Balthier growled. "If you want to be using anyone's shadow, use mine."

Balthier and Moonhunter got into the helicab and Balthier gave directions to a house just a block south of the one we were actually heading to. Once we arrived, Balthier paid the helicab driver and they got out quietly, as if they were just average ordinary passengers. Anything to not make themselves memorable so the driver would not be able to identify them later.

They pretended to go up the walk to the house until the delivery car pulled away and was halfway down the street. Then, Balthier and Moonhunter ran around the side of the house to the backyard. They jumped over the fence and ran through the yards, making a straight line to the house we were actually looking for. Balthier jumped and scaled the side of the house up to the roof. From here, we had a good advanced point to watch our prey.

I stepped warily out of Moonhunter's shadow and hoped I wouldn't slide off the roof. They had a lot less to worry about up here than I did and I certainly didn't want to slip off.

The house, in fact the whole neighborhood, seemed quiet

as we watched. Balthier pulled up floor plans he'd been able to find on his tablet while in route here and we matched it to what we saw of the house. We were too far away for them to sense any other novihomidraks, other than to know there were some in the vicinity. I could pinpoint at least six energies when I focused away from them and onto the house.

"Does she have the orb in the house?" I directed my question mostly at Balthier.

"The house is shielded." He shook his head as he answered. "Besides, with all the novies in there, it would be hard to find a sense of the orb within all the other vibrations."

"The Humline also doesn't say that it was brought here," Moonhunter added.

"So, we'll only know then by going in the house," I commented without it being a question but still wanting their confirmation.

"If she had never seen Moonhunter's face, we could've walked up there and said that we needed to have a meeting with her," Balthier said. There was an inflection on his tone which made me wonder if he thought that this was all my fault. At least he was forthcoming with a suggestion. "I could talk to her about something I'll have to dream up while Moonhunter searches the Humline and you look for its energy."

"She may have seen Moonhunter's face, but she didn't see yours. What if you went to her with a concern that your apprentice was hanging out with a ninja? Those implications alone could be scandalous. She knows that he wasn't acting alone."

Balthier's lips puckered as he sank into the deep concentration of thinking about what all that story would entail and what the other inferences behind it might be. With all the effort he was putting into it, it seemed like he wanted to be rubbing his chin thoughtfully as well. To my disappointment, he didn't. Instead, he reached into his pouch and pulled out the two little golden containers I'd given him when the novi-homidraks had accepted the mission. "That might at least get me in the door," he said. "These might help too, if they really are influence energy as you said."

He still didn't quite trust me about the energy balls. "They are," I confirmed.

"What about the two of you?"

I tried hard not to smile, but it was impossible, especially when I saw the shiver go through Balthier's shoulders. "He's working with a soulcolist ninja," I said. "If that's the story, then let us leave our clever tricks to ourselves. Moonhunter hired me to get the statue back. He could've easily spoken to me in the garden, if I had chosen to show myself at that time or if he had picked up my presence. Upon hearing of it being stolen, he sought me out and hired me to get the orb back. That will be our half of the story." I looked at Moonhunter who had a stoic face, but he nodded his agreement. Then I continued, "I have a few ideas for getting us inside. But if you don't know about them, Balthier, then your shock will be genuine. You go do your thing, and we'll break in."

"So when do I say was the last time I saw him?"

"We don't want her to know that the two of you were even together back in the saperes' temple, so how about you say that he ran off right after the last mission? You had suspected that he was up to something, and had tried to follow, but he disappeared and even though you waited for nearly half a day, he never showed up at the ship for the return voyage. You had to leave without him."

"Then how do I explain showing up on her doorstep? How likely is it that out of a random group of seventy-two Dragon Council members, I would just happen to pick her?"

"You work well with the Humline, don't you? You just tell

her that you had a feeling from the Humline that she was the one that you needed to speak with. Good enough?"

Balthier still seemed a little dismayed at this portion of the plan, but he consented. He pushed to his feet. "Okay, see you guys over there."

He gave one final look at Moonhunter, then stepped off the roof. Landing on the ground in a crouch, he stood and walked across the street to the house of the Dragon Council member.

Moonhunter turned his gaze to me, excitement fully grown in his eyes now. He'd done well to hold it back while Balthier was here, but with his master now gone, Moonhunter wanted to explore the exciting possibilities. "So what are we going to do? What's our plan?"

I hesitated to tell him too much right now, but I knew I had to keep him engaged and prepared for what was to come. It might be the only way that he would forgive me later. "It's going to take a lot of Humline work," I told him. "You'll need to stay in nearly constant contact with it, monitoring it. I'll watch for the more subtle energy ripples. I think between the two of us, we'll know well in advance of what we're supposed to do and of people coming our way. When we get over there, I'll pull you into the shadows with me and we'll be able to sneak through the house. All right?"

Moonhunter nodded. He blinked and I knew he was showing off his red dragon lids which covered his normally brown eyes. "Let's do this," he announced.

I stepped into his shadow, letting him taking me down off the roof with his own energy since he could just step off of it. Had I tried to do the same in my physical form, I would have broken a leg. After Moonhunter jogged across the street, I split off from him.

"Come on." I gestured for Moonhunter to follow, then I began a crouching run along the line of bushes beside the house. We soon came to a back entrance door. I looked to Moonhunter, knowing this was one area that might be his specialty. "Is the door going to be locked or not when I try it," I asked him.

I saw Moonhunter's eyes flicker, that certain little jerk that told me that he had switched to looking to the Humline for information. "It's unlocked," he said with a smile. "Why do I sense that we would make a great pair of burglars together?"

"A novihomidrak and a soulcolist ninja working together, partners in crime. That's something that would probably terrify the universe." I did have to admit, the thought did have a certain appeal. Ninjas were already known to play by their own rules and to walk a certain line that most cultures found publicly unacceptable.

I turned to face Moonhunter directly. "Ninjas have the ability to pull their victims into the shadows where no one can see them being stabbed or whatever the ninja is going to do to them. I'm telling you this because it's going to feel like you have chaos energy all around you. Your novihomidrak senses are going to be alarmed." It's what I hadn't wanted to tell him before, especially since I'd be taking him much deeper than the shadows, but he had no need to know that. Not that anyone could ever truly be prepared for the slender line known as the Unmasked between the physical world and the pure chaos of the universe. "I want you to keep your head and fight your aspects from coming out. Do you think you can do that for me?" Asking a novihomidrak to fight his very instinct was the most somber I felt I had been in quite some time. But I needed to impress upon him the severity of the situation; I certainly had no desire to be ripped apart by a novihomidrak.

"I think I can manage," he said.

"Just promise me not to panic. You need to stay calm for

me." Unlike so many other melodramatic scenes, I knew better than to ask him if he trusted me. He was a novihomidrak; of course he didn't trust me. Anyone smart would never trust a ninja.

I didn't wait for any affirmation from Moonhunter as I slipped into the shadows and came up behind him. Before he had a chance to realize what was going on, I reached one hand around him and covered his third eye while my other hand materialized right inside him to touch his heart. I pulled him into the deep, ethereal darkness of the Unmasked.

With Moonhunter gone from physical existence to being somewhere where chaos and dark energy reigned, I shifted back to the real world and opened the door. I didn't even bother to look around or inside, I just went back to the shadows and slipped through the opening of the door.

The room smelled of linen and laundry soap. Three of the five big machines were swirling a wash around inside them. Two others sat against the other wall and hummed as it tossed its contents around and around.

I felt Moonhunter resisting in the Unmasked. I clamped a shell around his energy, hoping that I could relieve his distress. Pulling a novihomidrak in that deeply was definitely not one of the smartest things I had ever done. It felt rather reckless. In fact, I'm sure that every honored ninja before me would be most displeased by my actions right now. Oh well, I had to get the orb, and I needed Moonhunter for that. There was no other way to get him inside. The Dragon Council member would know, would sense Moonhunter as soon as we entered her domain. Even with Balthier there, she would not be fooled. I could not reveal Moonhunter's presence until the last moment. However, that meant keeping him in the arena of chaos for far longer than I wished.

Traveling in the shadows with a living creature felt almost like swimming in very heavy water. The speed one moved through the shadows depended on how fast the ninja was moving when entering the shadows. Since I'd been walking cautiously and slowly, I had to keep grabbing the energy of objects in the room and hauling myself along with them.

I continued moving along, from one room to another, hiding in the shadows. After so many years, the abrasion of being in the shadows no longer unsettled me. Chaos energy swirled around in the dark, but it didn't bother me as much as it was agitating Moonhunter even in his protective shell. Chaos was nothing but another energy to work with, and even though the novihomidrak saw that energy as evil and destructive, there was nothing quite so simple in the world. Sometimes, things need to be destroyed or torn down to make way for the new.

Still holding onto his vexed energy from the Unmasked while dealing with the heavy oppressiveness of the shadows, I tired. There were better ways to have done this, but those weren't even options, so I knew I was best not to dwell on them.

Knowing that I needed to know where the orb was and that only Moonhunter's connection would lead me directly to it, I knew I had to get Moonhunter out of the chaos before he did something foolish. In his struggling state, there was no way he would be able to focus, or even be able to understand that he was looking for the orb. I needed to get him out of the Unmasked and quickly.

I reached out with my energy to search for the life force of other living beings within the house. There were a lot of them, and not all of them were completely human. I suspected that there were other novihomidraks in the house. It would certainly make this even more difficult. On the other hand, would the appearance of two more noviho-midraks, especially considering Balthier was arriving unan-nounced, make that much of a ripple? In an area full of novihomidraks, would they even be able to sense the addition of two more?

I stepped from the shadows moving into a concealment phase, which camouflaged me against the wall. I waited, listened. No shrieks of outrage went up, no cries of alarm, so I had to assume that the novihomidraks hadn't sensed me appear. Granted, being a ninja, I had already worked my energy to near nothingness. It made hunting targets easier when they couldn't sense you coming. It made working out the bumps in the Humline simpler to correct when you had no tangles or knots in your own lifeforce.

I decided to try to see if I could pull Moonhunter out of the Unmasked here. Both of us would be aware if someone was coming.

I had to step back into the shadows just deep enough to remove Moonhunter's energy from the shell. He struggled in my grip, fighting hard to tear free. I yanked him from the Unmasked.

I quickly pulled my hand from within his chest releasing his heart, and shook my hand off his third eye. Then I jumped back, waiting for the reaction.

Moonhunter hissed, but none of his dragon aspects appeared. He blinked and looked around. Then, seeing me, he asked, "How far in the house are we?"

I felt extremely pleased. With the exception of his snarl, Moonhunter had maintained control of himself. I would have to remember to tell Balthier how well-trained his apprentice was. "This place is huge. I've only gotten us inside and to a portion of the house that seems fairly quiet. The rest of the house will not be so vacant."

I saw Moonhunter's gaze shift, that tiny little flicker, and felt the ripple of his connection with everything.

"Is the orb here?" I asked, half afraid that the question would come with a negative response.

"It's not here," he said, reaffirming my fears.

"Not here," I protested, still wanting the words to be otherwise. "Is there any trace of it, or any indication of what she did with it? Is there any way we can track it?"

Moonhunter waited, or to me that's what it felt like. I knew he was searching, looking desperately for anything in the Humline of this world. When his gaze finally focused on me, he just shook his head.

"So all this has been for not," I knew that wishing and hoping wouldn't change the circumstances. Still, it also didn't improve my sour feelings. "It was here. We knew it was here."

Moonhunter's head lifted, then he reached out and pinched the fabric of my shirt sleeve. He gave a slight tug. "We need to be going," he said firmly.

He was right. People were coming. We ran out through the laundry room and did not stop until we were back across the street. Hiding in the shadows of the trimmed hedges, we crouched and waited for Balthier. We wondered how long we should give him.

Just as I was about to tell Moonhunter to search for Balthier on the Humline to make sure that he was okay, Balthier rounded the corner and crouched down beside us.

"That lady's a crafty one," Balthier grumbled. "She's got at least a dozen novies working for her, and that's just in the house alone. As the maid took me in to see her, I interrupted a conversation about payroll. I didn't hear enough of the conversation to be able to figure out anything more."

"Did you ask her about the orb? Maybe she had a clue as to why Moonhunter would be chasing it."

"She told me that she has no idea of what I'm talking about. Did you really expect her to answer otherwise?"

"So what we do now? I take it that you don't want to interrogate a novihomidrak on the Dragon Council." A part of me wished that my words would stoke Balthier's anger. I felt like it was time to start taking things out, to bring on the pain.

"Not if I can avoid it. We can't even be certain that it's her. It doesn't make sense that she would reveal herself so easily to us. A Necronosti is not going to come right out and show you who they are. This could be someone who wanted to entirely throw us off track and send us on an irrelevant hunt."

I wanted to pound something.

"Let's go back to the ship," Balthier said. "If nothing else, she reminded me of an option that we might try."

"Really?"

Balthier stood. "Yeah, and this might just work, if my ship hasn't been impounded already."

Armed security stood at the entryway to the landing docks, rifle barrels braced against the guards' chests as they watched all the people coming and going.

"Dang, I was hoping this would be easy," Balthier growled. "I forgot about the magic dampeners. Guess we get a little physical."

"Boys, boys," I said, "working out kinks in the Humline is my specialty."

Balthier's hand landed on my shoulder. "If I wanted people to die, I could do that myself. I'm not afraid to tear into someone."

"And I was thinking that we could do this without killing anyone. Besides, my powers aren't dependent upon magic."

"Can you take our energies like you did when you got me into the house?" Moonhunter asked, trying to be helpful as I started to walk away from them.

I turned, walking backwards as I continued. I couldn't help my smile at Moonhunter's offer. "Holding onto the energy of one novihomidrak was hard enough. While I know you're well enough trained to not rip everything apart when you come out, I somehow suspect your master wouldn't be as forgiving." I winked.

"What is she up to?" I heard Balthier ask Moonhunter as I got further from them.

I stepped into the shadows of a person approaching the entryway. As the host of my presence walked by the security detail, I hopped to the shadow of the nearest man.

The guard's eyes searched everyone coming toward the doorway, mainly concentrating on their faces. He'd been shown pictures of the two novihomidraks to search for: a grizzly old man with a graying beard and a young, fresh faced boy. They may or may not be together. They had no other way of detecting them.

I had to wait, sliding harshly along the shadow of the building, in order to get to where I could jump into the shadow of someone exiting.

My new host turned in the wrong direction and I had to vacate the shadow. The person never noticed me step away from them. I hurried back around to where Balthier and Moonhunter waited.

"They are looking for you, but they have no other ways to identify you other than by your faces. They haven't even been told that you are novihomidraks." I almost felt a pity for the guards, who would have been in for a surprise if they had tried to apprehend these two. "I have a plan for getting us inside."

"Great, but then what about getting us through and to my ship? We don't have a manifest or loading tickets because we had to get through the building so fast before. They certainly aren't going to let us just walk on out to our ship, especially since they will be guarding that as well."

I couldn't help the sour look I knew had to be on my face as I tilted my head to look at Balthier. "If the orb had been at the house, how would you have gotten back to your ship then?"

One side of Balthier's mouth lifted a little higher than the other as he smiled and said, "I figured we'd be leaving this planet like we do most others: in a crazy, mad, fighting hurry."

Moonhunter laughed as if backing up his master's words.

"This just feels wrong, walking in and trying to do it the natural and normal way," Balthier continued.

"It won't be natural or normal, I promise." I placed my hands on each of them.

"Wait! What?" Balthier shouted as a tingle emanated from my hand and ran through him.

"Look at you," Moonhunter cried out, pointing at Balthier. "You're an old woman!"

Balthier looked down, but I knew that all he could really see was his flowery dress on very old pink and gray material. The little yellow centers of the flowers seemed to shine back. Paisley designs rose into the fabric.

"Come now, Moonhunter," I said, reaching out for Balthier's hand. "We must take your grandmother inside."

"Grandmother?" Balthier looked at Moonhunter and gasped.

Moonhunter now looked like a little girl with curly waves, very reminiscent of the boy I'd seen in his subconscious sitting by the well. I admit that he still looked so cute that I wanted to kiss his adorable little cheeks.

"Holy mother—"

"Relax," I said quickly before Balthier's dragon aspects manifested and ruined my illusion. "I've only manipulated your physical energy. You both can live like this for a few minutes. One rule though: we have to maintain physical contact; if you break away from me, we have to touch again within seven seconds or you will change back."

"I don't know why you had to make me an old woman.

Certainly a strapping young man would've worked as an adequate disguise," Balthier grumbled.

"No, it wouldn't. They're looking for a young man. The last thing they are looking for is an old woman, her daughter, and her granddaughter."

"Great." Balthier limped along, attempting to avoid Moonhunter, who tried really hard to grasp onto Balthier's hand. Moonhunter finally managed it and began swinging their hands in rhythm with their walking pace. Moonhunter obviously enjoyed this much more than Balthier, who growled something under his breath.

"Come now, Mother. It won't be nearly as bad as you think. People travel every day." I said it loudly enough so that anyone standing nearby would just think that we were an ordinary family heading out on vacation.

As we headed into the terminal, I picked up some newspaper and began to fold sections of it up into trifolds. As I made each one, I thought about it being white with tight printed lines. The molecules settled into the new pattern that I set for them. Soon, I held onto tickets that said that they were for Alma Stock, Emily Stock, and Breanna Stock. I had no idea what their gate numbering system was here, but I took a chance, considering that this was one of the Dragon Council worlds, that it was a standardized system. I folded a fourth piece of paper and shifted the molecules on this to certify that Emily Stock was a certified shuttlecraft pilot. I left it over to the Onesong to make it look real enough that we would pass through security. I felt out along the Humline and did not see or feel any tangles in our lines. So far everything was working out beautifully.

Security had been tightened inside as well. As we passed by a large window that looked out onto the landing docks, I saw Balthier's ship patrolled by four more guards.

"There's certainly an awful lot of artillery considering that the orb wasn't even on this planet. Maybe I should've just signed the form and avoided all this conflict." Balthier looked around at all the armed guards and pushed in closer to me.

I patted the aged and wrinkled hand. "If the Humline wanted you to do that, wouldn't you have received indications sooner?"

Balthier knew I was right and cast a sharp eyed glare at me. He would've made a scary old woman.

As we approached the check-in station, I felt a ripple of hesitation go through my energy. There was a tangle. I squeezed Moonhunter's hand. "I need your help. Be cute."

Moonhunter nodded. I couldn't actually let the lady at the station take our tickets. I had to maintain contact with them, somehow.

"Hi y'all," the lady of the station said cheerfully. "Where y'all going to?"

"Off world," Balthier grunted.

"Oh, Mama, it won't be that bad."

Balthier glared first at me, then turned his irritated look to the woman at the counter. "I hate vacations. I'd rather just stay home and watch my tele-shows."

Somehow, I really did suspect that Balthier hated vacations. He probably wasn't acting that hard.

"I know what you mean." The girl giggled.

"Can my daughter scan our tickets?" I asked in the most genteel voice that I could muster.

"Well, I really don't know. It's really against company policy."

Moonhunter danced on his toes. "Please," he begged. He really would've made an adorable little girl.

"Well, maybe just one," the girl said.

"Oh, goodie," Moonhunter said as he raised his arms for me to lift him since he was too short to see up on top of the girl's counter. I knew I was in trouble. Just because I had changed their physical appearance didn't mean their mass had changed as well. Moonhunter would weigh just as much as his seventeen-year-old self. I turned to Balthier. "Mama, can you lift her up?"

"Seriously?" Balthier growled.

The woman also seemed shocked by my request. But Balthier shuffled around behind Moonhunter and the old grandmother easily lifted the little girl. I tried to give a soft smile to the woman behind the counter, but she still shivered. "In our family, we want to stay active late into life." I put my hand on Balthier's shoulder.

"Scan the ticket already!"

That prompted the woman into action. She directed Moonhunter to place the ticket under the scanner. It beeped. Moonhunter giggled with delight. "Again!"

The woman looked around. "Okay, one more time."

Moonhunter scanned the second ticket. The machine beeped for a second time.

I felt nerves growing in my stomach.

"Last one," Moonhunter said.

He slid the ticket under the machine. It issued a negative mechanical growl.

"Oh, dear," the woman said. "Here, let me give it a go."

Before Moonhunter could pull it away from her, she snatched the ticket from his hand and went to scan it.

Seven seconds.

The red line of the scanner went over the varied black lines of the ticket. It again gave the lower toned, angry beep.

Six seconds.

I nudged Balthier to set Moonhunter down.

Five seconds.

The woman set the paper on the counter and tried to smooth is out as if that would make it scan any better.

Four seconds.

She slid it back under the scanner only to receive its denial again.

Three seconds.

I tried to reach for it. She was already repeating her movements to smooth the paper out. I wanted to ask if she really saw a bend in it, but I had to stay pleasant; something about catching more flies with honey than vinegar.

Two seconds.

"Can I see that for just a moment?" I ask. If I could just touch it, it would reset the time we had. "I was afraid that it hadn't printed correctly." As if my explanation would help.

One second.

She began to hand it back to me.

I almost had it.

"Wh-what?" she said, nearly dropping the paper as if had burned her. The bright, colorful ink of the ads rose to the surface, bleeding madly over the white.

"Never mind," I said. Then to Balthier and Moonhunter, who I only now realized I hadn't touched in the same amount of time, I added, "Run!"

"It's them," the girl shouted. "They're over here."

Security guards raced toward us.

From the large windows, I could see the shadow of the building extending out over the asphalt of the landing area. A long stretch of shadow ran over the floor ahead, going right to the window.

"Keep your pace up like you're going to plow through them," I shouted to Moonhunter and Balthier as I positioned myself between them just slightly behind.

The guards raised their pistols. Laser or bullet, I wasn't sure and I didn't want to find out.

I damned the fact that the docking pad was off to the right. I had to look at it through the large glass windows while I stayed mindful of the novihomidraks.

"If you're going to do –" Balthier screamed, but it cut short as I reached out and touched their backs.

Shots fired.

Then we were on the asphalt as if we hadn't missed a beat.

The security detail around the ship looked up and tightened their grips on their semi-automatic weapons.

"Can you get us into the ship?" Balthier asked.

The shadows extending along the asphalt this far from the ship were scarce. Getting closer would be best. "Keep running." We needed a few more steps.

The guards ahead of us raised their weapons. Would they really fire toward the terminal?

I had no choice. We needed to get to the shadows.

What were the chances that security's weapons were novi-homidrak forged? Probably pretty good considering this was the very city where a member of the Dragon Council lived.

I saw it: the shadow that would take us right to the ship. I reached out for Moonhunter and Balthier, stretching beyond my means.

Stumbling, my fingers fell short.

I propelled myself forward a second time. Balthier jumped in front of Moonhunter. I compensated for the sudden move. The hand reaching for Moonhunter jammed against his back. Searing pain flared up into my shoulder.

Rapid fire vibrated in my ears.

Then it stopped and we were piled in a heap on the floor of the ship. Balthier groaned. "Moon, are you okay?" he asked.

"Yeah, I can move."

I figured the reply had to come from Moonhunter, though I wasn't really orientated enough to know where the voice had come from.

"Get to the controls and get this bird in the air," Balthier said. "I'm gonna need a moment."

Moonhunter shoved at me as he got up. Miscellaneous body pieces pushed around.

Then I realized the ship was being fired upon.

I rolled away from Balthier as Moonhunter went for the cabin.

"Get the shields up first," Balthier hollered.

"Done." Moonhunter's voice echoed from the compartment out into the hallway where we were.

Balthier still hadn't gotten up. Instead, he lay curled up in a fetal position on his side with his arms doubled around him.

I knelt down beside him. "Were they novihomidrak forged weapons? Are you injured?"

"You're not so lucky," Balthier moaned. "Not novi forged, but that doesn't mean the air pellets didn't pack a wallop! Now get away and give me a moment's peace, would ya?"

I stood and started to head toward the cabin where Moonhunter sat at the flight controls. I felt the ship beginning to lift beneath my feet. I stumbled into a chair.

"Not good," Moonhunter said. "Balthier, hold onto something back there."

I felt what Moonhunter referred to in the next moment as the energy of our newest predicament developed. A missile headed in our direction. I briefly wondered if Moonhunter and Balthier would survive landing on the docking pad below if the ship disintegrated from around us. I knew I wouldn't survive.

The ship yawed enough that I thought we'd end up in a barrel roll, but Moonhunter kept it together even while the engines died out. We didn't have enough altitude to be carrying on with stunts. Moonhunter stomped on a pedal beneath his left foot and slammed his hand against a button on the right. The engines kicked back in. The shipped stuttered, but surged forward. He pulled the steering hard to the right.

"Yes!" Moonhunter hissed, making a quick, triumphant fist.

Out the front window, I saw the missile soar right in front of us.

Moonhunter leaned toward me, smiled, then spoke in a low voice, "That's why Balthier lets me fly when we're in danger. Leave it to him to fake an injury."

"I heard that," Balthier said behind us as he leaned against the doorway, one arm still crossed over his stomach. "Now get outta my chair."

Moonhunter grinned as he obliged. "Sure, now that the danger is over."

I wished I could join in their frivolity, but the situation overshadowed any amusement I might have. We were back to having no leads on the orb. Worse, I knew that I'd put the novihomidraks in danger with the Dragon Council. It was only a matter of time until the terminal's security department reviewed the cams and identified who and what they were. Then the Dragon Council member on that planet, the potential Necronosti, would know that Balthier had lied to her about Moonhunter. She would not be happy and that would be an understatement, especially if she was as dangerous as I suspected her to be.

I rose from the co-pilot chair. "Excuse me." I headed for the door.

Moonhunter followed me out in the hallway. "Are you okay?"

I tried to give him a reassured look without smiling, a very hard task that I certainly didn't complete well. "I will be once we pick up the trail of the orb again."

Moonhunter suspected the half-truth of my words. "Balthier said he had an idea to do that. I'm sure that once we're safely away from the planet, he'll clue us in on that plan."

I nodded. "I think I will go and rest until then."

"Okay. I'll see you in a bit then."

I turned away from him and went to the room where I'd woken up. It felt like forever ago. I locked the door behind me and sat on the narrow bed wishing I could cry, but I had no tears. Only depression.

None of this would have happened if I'd just stepped from the shadows when I first saw Moonhunter looking at the orb and told him to take it. I'd felt it howling for him and I had stood by and done nothing. Now, I could still feel its yearning sadness. I didn't know how much of that was the memory of enduring the orb's years of lamenting or if I really did feel it. Maybe my own emotions were involved in it. After all, I had safeguarded the orb for so long that it had become routine, until Moonhunter had come along and reawakened my appreciation for what I protected. The way he stared at it, watched the light playing on the surface; those actions wiped the sleep from my days and made me long for each sunrise.

I buried my head in my hands, wishing I never had to get up.

"Past-master Calliesar," a voice said as a female appeared in the room before me, "I have been sent to issue you with a cease and desist order." The ninja spread her feet apart to shoulder-width and placed her relaxed hands upside-down near her hips. In one hand, she loosely held a rolled up scroll sealed with wax.

Yeah, my day was not going to end well.

The ninja stepped forward and extended the scroll toward me, standing there like a statue until I took it from her. "You have failed in your duty. You must return immediately and explain your actions."

"What actions am I being accused of?" I slid my finger beneath the wax seal and unfurled the message. I read the list aloud. "Failing in my guardianship of the stardust orb, check.

Certainly not a proud moment for me. Won't a 'I'm sorry' suffice?"

The ninja's face didn't reflect any amusement at my jest.

"Okay." I looked back down at the writing. "Not reporting said offense to the Black Nights. Check. I hadn't done that either. Enlisting the help of a novihomidrak. Actually, I asked for the help of two of them. You'll let the Black Nights know of their mistake, won't you? Oh, wait..." I paused slightly as I continued reading the list of charges, surprised, "dragging two novihomidraks through chaos on multiple occasions. Wow, they caught onto that one quickly, but didn't catch their prior error? Weird, don't you think?"

The ninja exhaled a deep sigh in which she pursed her lips tightly together. She looked tired. Of course, she had just shadowwalked with extreme calculations to catch a ship traveling in space. Even if we were still in the high atmosphere of the planet, space would have really challenged her skills. "Past-master..." she began with extreme patience.

Then, two angry novihomidraks appeared in the doorway.

I barely heard the override code beeping right before the lock clicked open. Balthier and Moonhunter hissed, each with their red dragon lids down and long teeth extended.

"Woah!" I jumped up off the bed and circled around the ninja. I held my arms out to protect her behind me. And even as I did the action, a part of my mind wondered why and screamed at me that I was being foolish.

Never turn your back to a ninja.

I knew this.

I remembered too late.

One of her hands reached inside me and touched my heart while the other covered my third eye. Blind and unfeeling, she led me into darkness.

A hand grabbed my arm as I fell backwards. I held on. Claws dug into my skin. I didn't care about the pain as Moonhunter tried to yank me free from the grasp of the ninja. If I got dragged into the Shadows, I might not make it out alive.

Fingers around my astral heart clenched tighter. I screamed, but here there was no sound. Only an explosion of light and the taste of fresh cinnamon.

The ninja flinched.

In that split-second, I broke away and I felt forward from Moonhunter hauling me out. I staggered into him. He caught me and the wall caught him. As I pushed myself away from Moonhunter, I looked around to Balthier. "What happened?" I asked.

"A good shot, considering I had to guess your location." Balthier pulled a cloth from his pocket and began to wipe down the long silver-colored barrel of his pistol. "Now, mind telling us what that was all about?"

"I'm to report to the guild of the Black Nights." I didn't yet want to confess that the Black Nights had accused me of multiple counts of crimes which were indeed true. At this moment, I would be found guilty. I had to recover the orb if I had any hope at all of getting leniency with the Black Nights. "Ninjas are like ants; we're going to see a lot more of them now. We need to hurry and find the orb. This ninja shadowwalked right onto our ship. That means she was fast. The next one will be a little slower, but probably more cautious too."

"Does that mean you have a bounty on your head?" Balthier asked wisely.

Certainly a good question. Ninjas took various jobs to get the bounties they brought in more often than for the challenge of bringing in a difficult target. This one had called me past-master, which meant that my title still held weight to her. But it might not for another ninja, perhaps one in the pursuit only for the sake of the hunt.

Balthier held his pistol out on the cloth. "Vochey." His

pistol vanished. He tucked the cloth back into his pocket. "Guarding an object like the orb, you are probably very highly ranked. A crime like this does not look good. I'm guessing that means your bounty is pretty high, right?"

I met Balthier's gaze, then dropped mine to the floor. I knew that was all the answer he needed.

"Then we better get to this. Moon, let's go find you a comfortable chair."

A few moments later, Moonhunter sat back and closed his eyes. He twisted the laser pointer between his thumb and fingers.

"Now just relax," Balthier instructed. "Let the Onesong guide you."

A vast array of networks seemed to illuminate overhead. It looked like a giant white net as it pulled further back, beginning to look more like a sponge.

Moonhunter's forehead furrowed with concentration, and then smoothed as he relaxed, only to wrinkle once more as he oscillated back and forth between trying to focus and trying to remain calm and open. It seemed to be a continuous struggle within himself. He seemed completely torn on how to do this.

"You're not stepping outside of yourself this time, Moon," Balthier said. His voice, due to the natural gruffness of it, wasn't as soothing as I knew he wished it was. I wanted to speak the words to Moonhunter, but my energy would be a distraction. Besides, I was already doing what I could.

As Balthier projected a chart of the Wells on the ceiling of the spaceship, I worked at putting an optilet on the floor. The optilet is a simple geometric pattern which acts as an energy shield. I worked at making this one contain Moonhunter's energy only, which would serve to raise his own power and keep everything else out.

Granted, I was only really concerned about keeping the

Necronosti out. I doubted most of the energies that the optilet guarded against cared about a young man searching the Wells for a shiny orb. Most were hungry for other things, or knew well enough to be scared of this object and stay as far away from it as they could.

Still, after having another ninja shadowwalk right on board Balthier's ship, I didn't want to take any chances of anything else getting in.

Moonhunter's breathing slowed as he began to relax.

"You've got control of the chart now," Balthier said. Moonhunter nodded and began to roll a little ball on the laser pointer around with his thumb. It frantically zoomed all over the sponge-like netting cast on the ceiling.

Balthier stepped away, putting his back to the wall. He tucked a hand behind him, between the small of his back and the metal panel.

Areas of the netting lit up like fireworks exploding. They would grow very bright, then fade. The intensity of some of them stayed longer than others as Moonhunter zoomed in on that portion, then went back out. I couldn't help but to wonder, considering his precision, if Moonhunter could really see the projection. But his eyes were still closed and I didn't think the image was bright enough to see through his lids, unless of course he had his dragon lids down beneath and that gave him the ability to see through the thin layer of skin. I couldn't help but to be somewhat jealous if that was another ability that the novihomidraks had.

Moonhunter's thumb jerked and sent the projection zooming in on a particularly bright blue planet. The laser pointer clicked and a red dot appeared on a specific portion of the planet. "There! It's there."

Balthier pushed a button on the wall. "Image locked. I'm sending it to the navigation computer now. In a moment, we'll know where we're going. Good job, Moon."

Moonhunter opened his eyes and stared up at the blue planet nearly overwhelming its space on the ceiling. "They have it in the ruins of Pentra Sy," he added.

A chill went through me, more than just from Moonhunter's sense of knowing.

"Pentra Sy?" Balthier asked, obviously never having heard of the place.

But I had. "They slaughter dragons as sacrifices to their gods. The ruins were said to have been a thriving city until it was destroyed by novihomidraks several centuries ago."

"Why would someone go there with this orb?" I watched as understanding clarity reached Balthier's eyes and he finished, "Because the orb is really a dragon and they want to sacrifice it because it's a special birth."

I nodded. "Probably trying to restore their lost empire."

Moonhunter's breath shuddered through him as he stared at the round blue dot still on the ceiling. "It's so scared. So far away from where it needs to be."

"We'll get it, Moon. It'll be okay."

I wished I could hold with Balthier's confidence, but the thieves already had the orb on Pentra Sy. Our chance of making it there before they could do whatever evil they had in store for the orb was slim.

Balthier responded to a beep from the control panel and he scrolled through the message it displayed. "Course has been locked in, but we're picking up another ship on a similar flight pattern. Somehow, I don't think this is coincidence. We better prepare to fight our way out of interception."

The thing about this planet we were going to was that it was a free commerce world. In and of itself, that brought the good and bad. The good was that there was no landing port that we had to gain access through. The bad thing was that pirates and thieves waited both in the atmosphere and on the planet to overtake crafts with small crews and steal the cargo for their own benefit. Being a small ship, and thereby showing that we wouldn't have a large crew, we were most likely a target for any of the pirating companies who spotted us. Chances were also good that whoever had the orb also had the potential to hire one of these crews and specifically look out for a small ship. There was also a chance that they knew Balthier's transmitting number, especially if they had gained that on another world, like the one we'd just been on.

We'd have no idea just how much danger we were in until we got closer to the planet. Then, the firefights would begin.

The cabin of Balthier's ship had an extra fold-down seat with a harness, which Balthier roughly pointed at as he and Moonhunter took the pilot and copilot seats and strapped into their harnesses.

"Get locked in," Balthier told me. I would have much rather rejoined the shadows, but there was no certainty I'd be able to remain there if the ship began to rock violently. I took Balthier's suggestion.

"Here it comes," Moonhunter said, pointing quickly before his fingers returned to the console before him.

I followed the direction he'd indicated and saw a rather large craft bearing down on us. It couldn't have been scarier if it had actually had a black rectangle with a skull and cross-bones painted on the hull. Worse, the sight of it suddenly made me feel very old. As a younger ninja, I would have looked at this as a challenge and anticipated the skirmish. Now, I just wanted to get the orb without any altercations. Why couldn't we all play nicely together?

As my younger self, I could have done so much more here, worked so much energy. But this was not my mission.

It was Moonhunter's.

He needed to do this. He was the youth and he had to understand what he would become if he let himself stretch his wings and grow, like the rising light of day over the land.

I watched him work at the console, his concentration one of intense focus. Did he have any idea of what direction his life would take? He was Moonhunter and already the energies surrounding him spoke of greatness.

Balthier's ship sustained a hit and we began to spiral. The gravity of the planet caught the craft and dragged it downward.

Then the ship jolted. The harness cinched tight across my chest.

"We're caught in a tractor beam," Moonhunter said. "Trying to break free."

"Don't bother. That hit disabled our engines." Balthier unbuckled. "Let's prepare for the welcoming committee."

As he got out of his seat and looked to me, he asked, "Do you have any tricks up your sleeve which could help us overtake about a hundred or so humanoids?"

I thought he'd never ask. "That might be a bit much, but if you two can take on twenty of them or so..."

Balthier smiled. "We've got more than twenty."

"From the looks of their ship's weapons, we can bet they have energy weapons of some kind," Moonhunter added as he rose from his seat.

"I can definitely handle those," I said, unclipping my harness. As I stood, I evaporated into the shadows.

"I hate it when she does that," Balthier grumbled. "Gives me the willies."

Moonhunter chuckled as he followed Balthier from the cockpit.

After several more moments where the novihomidraks waited impatiently, the ship began to settle and still. Balthier moved toward the door. "I don't want them crackin' into my ship," he muttered with a look to Moonhunter.

He gave Balthier a nod of approval. "I'm ready. I'm sure Calliesar is too. Let's do this."

Balthier punched the button to open the door and then stepped out of the way in case one of their captors began firing shots into the ship. None came.

I slid out, staying in the shadowplane of the craft. Who I saw outside waiting for us stunned me. I tried to go back inside Balthier's ship, but already Baltheir was holding up his hand and signaling that he was coming out peacefully. I didn't want to step outside the shadows and give myself away, but I couldn't warn Balthier and Moonhunter either. My time window expired as Balthier came out.

"We surrender," Balthier began. The last part of the word faded as he saw who was on the landing deck of the capturing ship. "Verity!"

"Thank you for showing up, Balthier. I see you've found your lost apprentice too." She smiled and motioned for Moonhunter to come out too. "This makes things so much easier."

"How so?" Balthier asked in his gruff voice as he headed down the ramp as if he were coming casually out to greet a friend.

"Why, you stole the orb from me, of course, and were coming to Pentra Sy to sell it to pirates. I couldn't let that happen, so I had to kill you both. Such a shame." The smile dropped off of Verity's face. "Kill them."

From the shadows, I reached out and captured the energy gathering in each of their guns. With nowhere else to store the energy, I had no choice but to wrap it like wire around my arms. It sizzled on my skin. These were novihomidrak forged weapons and stronger than most. Still, when the wielders went to fire the guns, nothing discharged.

"What?" Verity shouted. "I said, kill them!"

Balthier and Moonhunter rushed for their captors. Some tried to scramble out of the novihomidraks' way while others tried to fire again. A few of those closest to the council woman revealed themselves to be novihomidraks as well and surged forward to take on Balthier and Moonhunter. Verity tried to make her escape around behind all of the fighting. I followed her, taking up one of the guns someone had dropped in their attempted getaway. It made my arm visible for a fraction of a second, but no one seemed to notice it or the gun that vanished with me into the shadows.

Moonhunter also noticed Verity trying to flee and pressed through the battle to follow her. As much as I wanted to beat him, I knew he would make it across to her before I could slide along the shadowplane of the walls to get to her.

She slipped into the next room and shut the metal door behind her. Moonhunter, rather than punching the panel and pulling out a fistful of circuitry and wires as I had expected, paused momentarily, his gaze upon the keypad. Then he dialed in a series of numbers and the door opened.

Verity waited beyond. "Clever, young novihomidrak, and very, very stupid. Vochey Labor." A bladed polearm appeared in her hands.

Moonhunter stopped a ways from her, holding his distance to one longer than her glaive. "Where is the orb?"

"You don't even know what it is that you're fighting for," she screamed at him.

"I know it's a special birth and that you're trying to keep the council from finding out about it. That's all I need to know."

"Because the right sapere needs to touch it and declare what it is. The council cannot be deemed smart enough to make that decision."

"But you can?" Moonhunter's voice was cool and calm, especially compared to the din of battle behind him.

"I can."

"With a sapere on your payroll, no doubt. You think that

you can control the right person and make the special birth what you would desire it to be?"

"I will. I'll be this dragon's novihomidrak."

Once again, Moonhunter seemed to be listening to something outside of himself. "You do it for the glory, not for the best interest of the Onesong."

"There is no difference," she spat.

"There is."

"Moonhunter!" Balthier screamed from the bay behind them.

I glanced back to see Balthier engaged with more enemies than he could handle. He needed help.

Moonhunter held up his arms. "Vochey Tranquility." His bow appeared already with an arrow notched on the string. He let it loose. The string snapped and the arrow flew.

"Moon!" Balthier hollered again.

Exiting the shadows, I turned before I saw if the arrow hit or not. Balthier needed help more than I needed to aid Moonhunter. I ran toward battle, letting the wires of energy surge back into the gun I held and began firing upon the novihomidraks attacking Balthier. As shots landed, body after body pirouetted and fell to the floor. I reached down as I passed them and collected their souls.

Balthier hissed in rage as he fought his way through the novihomidraks that remained. Though his age had to be great, he seemed far from out of the game. Good. Moonhunter still needed his guidance.

"Where did he go?" Balthier asked as we finished our enemies.

I looked back to see Verity's body on the floor, but Moonhunter wasn't nearby. Balthier began to run in the direction we'd last seen Moonhunter and I followed. As soon as we entered the hallway beyond the bay, we found the extending halls empty. Balthier spoke in dragon tongue, then began to rush off in a direction I had to guess that he'd picked from indications he'd gathered from the Onesong.

We came to an open doorway. The light illuminated sleeping quarters. Moonhunter was inside, sitting back on his heels on the floor. Before him was a black box lined with plush velvet so that it nestled the orb. The lid rested upturned on the floor beside him. He looked back at Balthier. "I've got it."

MOONHUNTER HELD the box and I stood nearby watching as Balthier shook hands with a man who had come up to us later and announced that he was the captain of the vessel that had captured us in the tractor beam. Captain he may claim to be, but pirate he certainly was. They'd had a long discussion, one in which I felt influence energy at work and knew that Balthier had opened one of the golden orbs I had used as payment to him, then the crew had set to work on fixing Balthier's ship.

Once repairs were made, Balthier hopped up the ramp onto his ship. "We're all ready to go," he proclaimed.

"Where are we going?" Moonhunter asked.

"We're going to take that somewhere safe," he said as he pointed to the black box Moonhunter had refused to let go of since he'd picked it up. "Plus we have a passenger who I'm sure would like dropped off somewhere."

"I will be going with you until we have the orb safely where it needs to be," I informed Balthier, who didn't look pleased about it, but didn't seem like he was ready to boot me off the ship here at Pentra Sy either. I knew I should be grateful for that. "I have the souls of the novihomidraks. I will release them at the shrine where we leave the orb. They will be home."

"We also have to talk to the Dragon Council about Verity's death. The captain will deliver the bodies of all the novihomidraks to the nearest council world," Balthier told us. Then he fixed Moonhunter with a hardened look. "But the council will have difficult questions for you."

Moonhunter nodded. He glanced down at the box gripped in his long fingers. I worried about the Dragon Council wanting retribution for Verity's death.

Balthier, too, had obviously been thinking the same thing. "It's what we do, Moon. We're novihomidraks, champions for the Onesong. When one of us goes bad, we can't have that. We certainly couldn't have her corrupting a dragon, let alone a special birth. There's already enough chaos and mayhem out there without a rogue novihomidrak adding to it." Balthier patted Moonhunter's shoulder as he walked by, heading for the cockpit. "Remember that and know it's the same reason we must now get the orb out of your reach. You still have lessons to learn."

"I just can't help feeling I'm losing out on an incredible adventure," Moonhunter moaned.

"You're not." Here's where I needed to step in. I touched Moonhunter's hand and gave him the energy the orb had been showing me over the years. "Wait for it to all come together as it should. It's stardust from near your home world. It will always call for you, and someday, you will be able to answer it."

Moonhunter's eyes widened and he smiled. "I trust the Onesong," he confirmed.

He sat back in the seat as Balthier prepared the ship for takeoff. Moonhunter took the lid off the box and stared at the glistening orb lying in the black fabric.

Balthier's ship went through the bay doors and exited into space, heading to the planet where they were to take the orb.

As Moonhunter watched the dragon egg within the box, a

bright shaft of sunlight came through one of the craft's side windows and lit across one side of Moonhunter's face. Like I had before, I watched the morning rays of the horizon play on Moonhunter's skin in much the same way it had on the monk statue which had once held the orb.

Three times in his travels had Moonhunter found the orb. Someday, when the time was right, it would find its way to Moonhunter again. For now, it had all the attention it needed.

MOONHUNTER'S STORY will continue in Dragons of Welldeep (coming soon). Sign up at www.dawnblair.com/newsletter for updates.

DAWN BLAIR

STARDUST

A WELLS OF THE ONESONG STORY

STARDUST

As a word that meant "wise one," Reila felt that the label of sapere didn't quite fit her and possibly never would. Why did she sit here trying to gain the title if she already knew she was doomed to fail? She looked down at the spiraling tattoo winding around her wrist as though it were further proof that she didn't belong here.

A muffled snicker came from one of her classmates while she tried to recall the answer to the question she'd just been asked. She didn't know who had made the sound. Then came another chuckle from someone else. Reila glanced back over her shoulder to see if she could tell who was laughing at her.

"Reila?" the sapere-san asked, making Reila feel even more uncomfortable.

"I... don't know," Reila stammered.

"You don't know," Sapere Juliac began, his voice holding a tone of disbelief, "the spell required to open the Wells?"

"Freak," she heard the whisper behind her.

Reila felt her chest beginning to get tight. She couldn't even get enough air to speak. "I -- I..."

As if the Onesong sensed her discomfort and wanted to

give her a way out, the chimes rang. Everybody including Reila grabbed their books and notes as they jumped from their desks and headed for the door.

"Vice Reila, can I see you for a moment?" Sapere Juliac demanded behind her.

Reila pretended not to hear him as she headed from the room. He called out her name again, but she was nearly to the door and almost truly didn't hear him over the clamor of her peers.

"I expect you know the spell by tomorrow," Juliac called out. By this time, she was out in the hallway. She didn't feel safe though until she was outside.

Once the light breeze hit her face, she began to relax. She made her way across the courtyard which joined the saperes' temple to the school, hurried by the fountain, and stopped beside the tall, stone pillars where the convergence of the Wells met this planet. She thought of the convergence like a belly button before the umbilical cord was tied off. This was where the universe touched her planet. She might not be able to recite the spell that would open the Wells, but she felt safe here.

She had let her guard down too soon.

Lon came up behind her and smacked her in the back of the head. Her loose brown hair fell into her face. She wiped a hand over her eyes, trying to remove strands of hair out of her lashes. Lon knocked her books and notes from her other hand.

"How do you even think you'll get to be a sapere?" he asked. "You wouldn't even know a dragon if one came up and spit in your face."

"Don't judge her living circumstances. Some people can't help being poor and stupid." This comment came from Vael as she walked past them. Vael with her graceful stride and long, curly blonde hair which hung in waves halfway down her back. Everything Vael was, Reila was not: beautiful, rich, loving parents... Vael added, "Magicless too."

Lon gave a little laugh at Vael's statement. "Yeah, but you think they wouldn't promote her along with the class if she isn't even capable of remembering the ceremonies. Was that some sort of pity vote for her?"

"I don't think anyone could've had pity for that odd little mouse. Maybe a dragon will eat her someday," Lon's friend, Traese, added. He knocked Lon's arm and continued walking along. "You think your mom's got snacks ready yet?"

"I certainly hope so," Lon said.

They rushed on, seeming to forget about Reila for the moment. She preferred it that way. She knelt down to collect her books and notes until the stream of people thinned out and she felt safe enough to rise without being noticed.

But as Reila walked on, none of their words bugged her more than that of the snacks. She could take the other teasing. But food...

There would be no snacks waiting for her. Just a room with a bed and a desk. After she dropped off her school items, her chores would need to be done. Once she'd finished with the daily cleaning of the shrine, she'd get her bowl of mush. Someday, she promised herself, she wouldn't be poor any longer. Someday she would outgrow her current living circumstances.

But how? She couldn't even remember what she needed to do as a sapere. Would they soon decide that training her was a waste of everyone's time?

Reila found herself walking down near the river. She sat down on a rock and bent over her books. She let her hair fall down around her face like a curtain to hide her tears.

How was she going to make it as a sapere? Unlike the other children, who had been favored by dragons in their youth and blessed with dragon magic, she had just been branded with the tattoo around her wrist and told that if she wanted to do something other than be a shrine worker for the rest of her life, she would have to become a sapere. Maybe she should have chosen the shrine. She already lived in poverty there.

At least she wasn't enslaved like her parents. That seemed to be the only thing worse that could happen to her. She had no idea what had happened to them after they were sold to pay their debts. It was illegal to sell children as young as she had been at the time, so her parents had left her at the shrine instead.

Reila knew she should be glad to serve at the shrine. She'd heard of other orphans who weren't so lucky. At least her parents hadn't been in debt to any wizards, so she hadn't had a curse placed on her head as well. She knew she could be worse off. Still, that didn't help her plight. If she didn't find some time to study, she was certain that they would never allow her to become a sapere. Her room had no light, and she had no money to buy candles or oil, and since chores began as soon as the sun rose and continued until the sunset when it finally became quiet at the shrine, she had no way of studying her notes and her books. How would she find a way?

Reila glanced at the river. How desperate was she? She put her books and notes down on the ground beside the rock and stood. Within three steps, she stood on the riverbank. Three steps more and she'd be within the fast current.

She looked down at the reflection of herself in the water. Long, straight, tangled brown hair surrounded her dirty face. She was looking scrappy again, she realized, thinking about how one of the saperes had once described her to Keeper Tjarsen. That was just moments before he promised to get Reila a hairbrush, which she hardly ever used. She reached up and brushed a strand of hair out of her face, catching sight of the twisting tattoo around her wrist as she did so. She hated that it had to be in her reflection as well.

She angrily wiped away the tears strolling down her cheeks. The drops flipped off her hand and plunged into the river. She saw her red eyes within the reflection. The image of her rippled as the water moved. The Keepers of the shrine warned all the orphans about the river's undertow. She thought they did that just to make sure they knew their options. Every year found two more orphans drowned. She thought she now understood, because sometimes being an orphan with no options meant that death was the best choice. At least you weren't here wasting your energy anymore. Your energy could go back to the Onesong, and maybe begin to dream of a new life again.

She hated the fact she was even contemplating ending her life. Her parents had tried so hard to save her. If she chose suicide as a way out, she would be throwing away everything they had done, even though that had never been enough. Why did they have to get into such debt as they had? Why couldn't they have chosen to fight for their lives harder? Why couldn't they have made better use of the energy that the Onesong had given them? She wondered if she would ever realize the answers or if they would ever make sense to her? Once her soul was no longer attached to this body, would it even matter?

A desperate part of her longed to know the solution to that question. She wondered if anyone had any answers to anything. There were times that she wondered if the noviho-midraks, those reborn from dragons which she occasionally served, had any more understanding of the universe at large than she did. It seemed like everyone was lost, trying to muddle through. Even the saperes, who were thought to be wise ones, didn't seem to have all the answers. Neither did the Keepers of the shrine. At least she could read. Many of the Keepers couldn't even do that much. That might have been the only reason they were trying to make her a sapere.

The cluster of agony within her chest seem to be easing a little bit. Maybe thinking about all this and realizing that no one had all the answers was giving her a bit of relief. She hoped so. If she could just find something to give her a reason to walk away from the water now, she might find the strength to wake up on this dimension another day. She so badly wanted out of this life. Three easy steps.

"Vice Reila!" came a woman's voice.

Reila turned around to see one of the Keepers up on the path waving her arms and trying to get Reila's attention. The woman's light orange dress swayed around her calves as her arm thrashed in the air.

Reila thought about not waving back, but knew she couldn't let the Keeper continue to swish back and forth like a landed fish. Reila stepped away from the water's edge, gathered her books and papers, and started the short, steep accent up the embankment.

Ureli, the woman in orange, waited with her lips pursed tightly together. "Reila, you really shouldn't go down there. You could break the straps on your sandals. Then where would you be?"

As if breaking the straps were the worst things that could happen to her standing at the water's edge, Reila thought. She'd been without shoes, both before her parents were sold away to the debtors' mines and after. Only when the frost had made a thick cover on the pathway between the shrine and the school had the Keepers thought to get her some shoes, and that was only after a sapere had complained about appearances. "I'm sorry, Keeper Ureli," Reila muttered, keeping her gaze downcast.

"Don't let it happen again."

"I won't." Reila, with her eyes lowered, couldn't help

looking at Ureli's sandals. The black shoes laced up around Ureli's calves. She couldn't see how high they went from her dress skirt cutting off the view.

"Come along now. We need to be getting back. We have a special novihomidrak coming though and all hands are needed to prepare the shrine and care for his needs."

Any strength Reila had left in her seemed to leave and lowered her shoulders as a result. She had definitely made her steps in the wrong direction. "I understand, Keeper."

"Good. Now do you know where the others are?"

Ureli thought the three children that went from the shrine to the sapere's temple for schooling were the best of friends. Well, two of them were. Reila tried to stay out of their way. She tried to stay out of everyone's way. The fewer people who noticed her meant the fewer people to mock her. "No, Keeper," Reila responded.

"Well, they must be around here somewhere." Ureli looked around as if the other two would just pop into existence before her. "Hurry on back to the shrine and let Keeper Tjarsen give you an assignment. I'll look for your friends."

Reila bent slightly at the waist and lowered her head even further in a half bow. "Yes, Keeper." Then Reila stood up straight and dashed around Ureli. She ran as fast as she could back to the shrine. The last person she wanted to be in trouble with was Keeper Tjarsen. If she were the last one to get an assignment, she might be cleaning out the commodes. She really would have wished she'd walked out into the river then; some of the older Keepers had issues with their functions, making their commodes stinky and messy. Quite often, they used the ones in the public areas rather than retiring to their own chambers first. Something about needing to go more often even though they ate so much less than everyone else. Another mystery of life.

The shine sat atop a small hill and a long staircase led the way up to it. Huge pillars guarded the outside and dwarfed the small door in the center.

As Reila approached, she saw several councilmen walking along the shaded path that led to the building which housed the members of the Dragon Council. Normally when they came over to the shrine for their daily work, they wore their normal sapere robes. Today, however, they were dressed in their good robes, which had braided cords hanging off the shoulders, high collars which indicated their rankings, and complete ritual jewelry.

If the Dragon Council was coming to the shrine dressed for ceremony, then the novihomidrak who was coming was very important, more than Reila realized before. She gulped, then hurried to a sprint knowing she had to get to the shrine faster.

When she got inside, the shrine was already abuzz. Apparently, the novihomidraks – yes, two of them – had arrived early. Reila hurried through the hallways, scanning each direction for Tjarsen.

What were two novihomidraks doing coming here? Was there impending danger for the planet? Reila suddenly wished she'd paid more attention to current events. She promised herself she'd do better in the future. She had to remember that her job, if she could make it to becoming a sapere, would depend upon it.

Reila came to a dead stop in one of the hallway intersections, backing up slowly out of the hallway, as Chief Keeper Kelty along with her entourage of Keepers and the two novihomidraks came down the hall.

"It is certainly a pleasure to meet you, Balthier, and your apprentice Moonhunter," Kelty said.

Reila shrank back, wishing that she could evaporate into the shadows nearby. She had nearly stepped in front of the novihomidraks. The older novihomidrak, obviously Balthier, had a graying beard and sharp, fierce eyes. His apprentice was no more than a boy just a few years older than herself. He was lean, like a wire, but his budding muscular development showed beneath the wheat colored tunic. He had long black hair, tied back, but it still hung in loose waves nearly to his waist. The young novihomidrak glanced to Reila and smiled.

Reila jumped back against the wall and pressed her hands against her chest. Novihomidraks weren't known for smiling at people. They would rather show you tooth and claw first. Of course, the boy was only an apprentice, not much different than herself. She was certain that his master would reprimand him later for the indiscretion.

Reila waited until everyone had passed and the footsteps had faded completely away before she continued her search for Tjarsen. She found him where she been expecting to find him, in between the kitchens and the meal hall, where preparations were hurriedly being made. She realized she hadn't even had time to drop off her books and notes. She dropped them down onto an unused counter and push them back against the wall, hoping that they wouldn't be in the way until she could retrieve them later. Then she hurried over to Tjarsen. "Keeper Ureli said that you needed everyone urgently."

Tjarsen had been looking right over her head, and glanced down now fiercely at the interruption. But when he realized who she was and that she must've run back from class in a hurry to get there, he softened. "Vice Reila, go and help make sure that everything is out. But by the time the dinner bell sounds, you need to be out of this room. Only Keepers will be allowed tonight."

"Of course." Reila did understand. "I saw the novihomidraks in the hallway."

"They're here?" he asked, surprised. Apparently everyone else in the shrine knew that the novihomidraks were here, but the news hadn't yet reached the kitchens. Tjarsen's eyes filled with panic as he looked up. He raised his hands and clapped them. Then he rushed around and hurried back for the kitchens, his shouted orders growing muffled as he went behind the thick stone walls.

Reila went into the meal hall where the tables were all lined with red cloths. Gold trim lined the edges. So, the visiting novihomidraks were from a Ch'bauldi dragon.

Bards, each with various musical instruments, set up by a wall in one corner near where the head of the table would be seated. Would Chief Keeper Kelty give up his position to the novihomidraks tonight? Reila wished she could be here. She could eat off the golden silverware a Keeper shoved in her hands to place around the table while the golden candlelight flickered off the crystal glasses. If she closed her eyes, she could smell the odor of the chickens roasting in the kitchens and imagined them out here being served.

As the bards tuned their instruments, she watched them. She wondered how hard it was to learn to play. Maybe she should ask? Could she even acquire an instrument? How expensive were they? Maybe she'd have better luck with music than her hopeless lessons to become a sapere.

"Reila," a Keeper shouted. "Quit daydreaming and get that table set."

"Yes, Keeper," Reila responded with a nod. She went back to work even as her heart sank further into her own blue river. She would never get out of here.

As final preparations were set, Tjarsen ordered Reila from the kitchens and back to her room. He shoved her bowl of mush into her hands as she snatched up her books and hurried away. As she headed toward her room, she realized it was still light for several more hours and that all the Keepers were occupied. She had no reason to go back to her room and who would know that she wasn't there.

Instead, she made her way out into the shrine's gardens, where she sat down on the one of the benches among the flowers.

First, she ate while the white mixture was still warm. Once it cooled, it had a tendency to harden and stick to the bowl. Afterwards, she cracked open her books and tried to study.

A butterfly danced a path along her vision and seemed to beckon her to follow. She set the book aside and followed the butterfly to the rose bush. She watched it land on flower after flower, touching the velvety petals.

Its wings were shimmery white, sparkling in the evening light, with blue, green, red, and yellow smearing over it as if it had been in a colorful rainstorm. Black legs crawled over the flowers.

Soon, Reila dared to see if the butterfly would step onto her finger. She reached up slowly.

The butterfly startled and took flight. She watched it fly over the shrine walls until it disappeared into the sky.

Her smile at watching it go faded as she wished she could so easily move on with her life. The only way she might escape these walls was if she studied. She hurried back to her books determined to study until sunset.

She placed the bowl on the ground and stretched out on the bench, holding her book above her to read it.

Her eyes began to droop. She was so use to doing her chores, eating, cleaning up from dinner, then going to bed. Now that the growls of her stomach were satisfied, even if she weren't full, she felt tired from her day of studies and chores.

She didn't even notice when she dropped the book down on her chest and fell asleep.

The cooling night air woke her. At first, she thought she'd fallen asleep on the bench by the river. The Keepers would not be pleased. But as she sat up, she realized she was in the shrine's garden. Her foot knocked against her bowl.

She had lost her free evening of study time.

Taking up her books and bowl, she made her way through the near blackness toward the shrine. At least she'd worked out here enough that she knew her way.

She slid the door open, stepped inside, and closed the door as quietly as she could. The halls of the shrine were quiet and Reila hoped that no Keepers roamed about now. Had the novihomidraks taken to their quarters already? If they were settled in for the night, then maybe the Keepers had also turned in.

Tiptoeing along, she thought about returning the bowl to the kitchen, but knew that someone might still be there cleaning up. If someone saw her awake and sneaking around, she'd either be in trouble or asked to help, neither of which she really wanted. She decided to head straight to her room instead.

Reila rounded the corner and came face to face with the boy novihomidrak.

"What are you doing here?" she asked rather abruptly. "Shouldn't you be with your master?"

He put a finger to his lips and pressed air against it. "Shh, I snuck out, okay? I want to do some exploring." His eyes, the color of soft chocolate, glanced each way down the hall-way, his head turning only a minimal amount, but Reila sensed that he was searching with more than just his gaze. He returned his attention to her. "You probably know your way around here quite well, don't you?"

She thought about saying that she was new here, but knew that she'd soon be confessing the truth to him if she did. "I've lived here almost my whole life," she admitted.

He seized her items from her, set them on a table there in

the hallway, then grinned as he grabbed her arm. "Great! Let's go."

Reila wanted to pull away. She wondered if he had claws or talons. A small whimper came from her throat as she realized she might very well find out soon.

"What's the quickest way out of here?" he asked. As he looked down the hallways, his head turned with short, predatorily movements. Reila saw his eyes had turned red and she shivered.

He tossed her a questioning gaze. "You act as if I'm going to eat you."

"Are you?" her voice issuing a small tremor.

He glanced her over, his forehead furrowing. "No!"

She wasn't certain if she should believe him.

"Look, I just want to go look around at your world, explore a little, have some fun," he explained, blinking his eyes. They returned to their normal human color. "I enjoy some company because local inhabitants always know the best places. But if you don't want to join me, then just show me how to get outside."

"I didn't think novihomidraks liked to hang out with humans," she whispered, still only finding that much sound.

He laughed. "It's usually the other way around; the humans don't like to hang out with novihomidraks. We're scary." He raised his hands above his head and curled his fingers like claws all while making a funny face at her.

Reila giggled.

"Yeah, it's funny, right? People are weird. I don't know why they think that novihomidraks don't still have the same needs and emotions as every other human."

"Okay," Reila muttered.

He paused. "Okay, what?"

"Let's go out, outside I mean." She felt a heated blush hit her cheeks and hoped he didn't see it. "My name is Reila."

"Reila," he repeated. "That's a beautiful name. Mine's Moonhunter. Dumb, huh? Who would hunt a moon?"

"No, I like it." She hesitated as they walked along, a question on the tip of her tongue and she wondered if she should ask it. She guessed that the worst that could happen would be that he'd eat her. Considering only a few hours ago she'd been contemplating walking into the river, what difference did it make? "Was that your name before you were dragon born?"

"I don't remember my human name," he answered, his voice completely flat and emotionless. While she hadn't known him long, to hear him completely as hard as steel made her wonder if she had crossed some line.

"I'm sorry," she apologized quickly. "I shouldn't have asked."

"Look, are we friends?" he asked.

She considered it for a moment. Friends with a novihomidrak. Was that even a possibility? "I guess," she responded, still not sure how she should answer or how she felt about it.

"Good. Then don't apologize for the question." They headed out of the shrine into the cool night. He continued, "Ask me anything you like. If I don't want to answer something, I won't and you'll respect that because we're friends. But I imagine that you want to get to know me as much as I want to get to know you and your world."

"What are novihomidraks doing here on my world?" The question spurt forth from her before she had the chance to think about it.

He grinned again, giving a small shake of his head. "We're just bringing an item to your world for safekeeping. There's no danger, at least not to you or your world. I do wish we didn't have to leave it, but our hands are tied in this circumstance. "

Reila felt like it was her turn to offer something up for him. "Where do you want to go?"

"Do you have somewhere where you go often?"

"The school," she replied, not sure she wanted to take him there. It seemed like a boring place to her.

"School? What do you learn there?" He seemed genuinely interested.

"I'm training to be a sapere."

"Really?" he asked with a huge smile.

"Yes." Now her voice was flat.

"So have I now touched on a subject best not followed?" Moonhunter leaned over slightly as if trying to read her better.

She involuntarily raised her wrist and she knew that he saw the tattoo there. "I wasn't favored by a dragon."

He reached over and took her hand in his. She flinched at the contact of skin on skin, but he held tightly onto her as if he'd expected her reaction. "Wow! We were so fated to meet," he said. Moonhunter stopped and examined her wrist and the tattoo around it. "I'm an oddity of a novihomidrak and you are an oddity of a sapere in training. I have several friends who are training to be saperes at the temple on my base world. What do they call trainees on this world?"

"A vice. It's short for novice, but they drop the first part of the word because they didn't want anyone trying to call themself a novi."

He smiled, catching her meaning. Novi, after all, were how some of the novihomidraks referred to themselves. "Funny. People are weird," he reiterated.

"Aren't they now?" she asked.

"I did say I was the oddity, didn't I? Yeah, well, I'm fascinated by how humans are human." He gestured toward the houses they walked by. "Everyone is having their own little adventure and creating their own masterpiece as the star of the show. It's how they react to it, how they go through their daily lives, which amazes me. To you, it's just what you do day in and day out. But to me, it's a different experience than what I have. I want to stop and look into the window of your life, just to see what it's like."

"Which makes you want to see the school where I go every day?"

"Yeah. Do you think we can get inside?"

The thought of breaking into the school made her stomach tremble with nerves. If the saperes caught her away from the shrine, forget that she was also with a novihomidrak, the Keepers wouldn't be happy. She hadn't anticipated Moonhunter wanting to go inside the school.

"Okay," he said before she had a chance to say anything, "another boundary. You don't want to get into trouble. I respect that."

He still hadn't released her hand and he gave one more look at the tattoo. She noticed that his eyes had changed to red again. "Oh, sweetheart," he said, "you may not have been favored by a dragon before, but you are kissed by the Onesong." She could scarcely believe his words. "I know you don't feel it yet, but you are loved."

His words almost brought her to tears. She certainly didn't feel very beloved by the universe. She wanted to deny his words, but the overpowering weight of her shame held her back. She couldn't admit everything to him.

He untied a pouch from his belt and handed it to her. "Please take this," he entreated as he handed the pouch to her in his cupped hands. "I know now why it was so important for me to come on this mission and why the Onesong urged me to meet you."

Curious, she took the pouch and looked inside. It was filled with little gemstones, all brightly polished and beautiful. They looked like little round bits of stardust. Tears started rolling down her cheeks as she realized the fortune she now held in her hands. "I can't accept this. My parents are in the debtors' mine. I'm only at the shrine because I had no other family to go to. I can't take this."

Moonhunter closed his hands over hers so that her fingers pressed against the gemstones within the leather pouch. "It's my earnings from the Dragon Council. But all my needs are already met, and I will earn more when I get back from this trip. Please, accept this offering as a patron's donation to your education as a sapere."

She wished she could look away from his brown eyes, but when she dared to try, the beautiful curls of his hair which framed his face captured her attention. He was the most beautiful boy she had ever seen and she understood why the dragon had wanted him. He was so beautiful, inside and out. He deserved his title as a novihomidrak. And here he was, selflessly helping her to gain her title as a sapere. How could she turn him away?

He moved his hands to embrace her head and wiped his thumbs against her cheek to take away the tears. "Following your path to become a sapere is the most important thing you can do right now," he told her. "Buy the oils or the candles that you need and any other supplies which will help you on that journey. I can't tell you why, but it is so very important to the Onesong that you do that. You have all that you need right there in your hands. Use it wisely."

She clutched the pouch close to her chest, knowing that his gesture of kindness toward her was worth so much more than the stones within the bag. "Thank you."

His brown eyes sparkled even in the dim light, looking up as though reading something over her head. "Your journey will be amazing. I wish I could be there with you. What an adventure you're going to have!"

She realized then what he was doing. He was reading her future from the Humline.

His gaze returned to her and locked with her eyes. "In

fact, you are going to do the very thing that Balthier and I can't do."

"What's that?" she asked.

"Have an amazing adventure." He grinned.

And now, she knew why novihomidraks were truly scary.

They spent a good portion of the night roaming the streets while she told him about the city where she lived and what happened there. They ended up on the bench by the river and she sat close to him for warmth. He seemed fascinated by her every story and begged for her to share more experiences until she was so tired she fell asleep against him. He must have carried her back and tucked her into bed, for she woke in her room the next morning to find the novihomidraks had already departed. Moonhunter's words stayed with her long after he'd left her world. She did her best to spend the fortune he had left with her wisely. She even took on odd jobs to earn money as her self-esteem built up and she settled into feeling more confident about herself and her skills.

At one point, she even wrote Moonhunter a note and asked the Dragon Council to see it delivered to him, though she wasn't sure they would let the letter through to him. She hoped he would be able to make it for her graduation. She never knew if her letter got delivered or not as she never received a reply. Maybe novihomidraks were never taught to read or write as their lives were already dedicated to other things. Rather than feeling depressed about it, she chose to believe that his faith in her never wavered and she continued on until the day she became a sapere.

Reila carried her head high as she walked down the hallways of the saperes' temple. She had earned this. She looked at her wrist, the tattoo no longer being an odd brand, but rather the proud reminder of her novihomidrak patron who had made this moment possible for her. Since she had no dragon's favor, she got to choose one in her heart. She had chosen the Ch'bauldi dragons. After today, she would use what remained of her funds to travel to the Ch'bauldi temple and begin her service there. She hoped that one day she would be honored enough to meet Moonhunter again. Since novihomidraks aged so slowly, would he still look like a boy? She knew she had grown much since their meeting. She wondered if he thought of her nearly as often as she thought of him. Once she was a sapere for the Ch'bauldi dragons, then maybe she would find a successful way to contact him to tell him thank you for all he had done for her. She wanted him to know that she had succeeded.

Unfortunately, right now, she was late. Realizing that she'd slowed down yet again, she picked up her pace. She'd stayed up too late, held up by company at the shrine which needed entertained, and her nearing graduation had been cause for celebration. It wasn't often that the Keepers had one of their own about to become a sapere, and the Keepers, the councilmen, and several other people had wanted to come and congratulate her. Since the party had been for her, her presence had kind of been required. Then, afterwards when she found a moment to excuse herself for the night, she went back to her room to yet again study the ritual for the ceremony of her titling. This was an important day, and she didn't want to mess it up. But because she'd stayed up so late, she hadn't heard the first bell of the morning. She slept to the second bell. That, and Keeper Ureli pounding at her door screaming for her to get up.

A strange growl sounded in a room off to her right. She knew she shouldn't concern herself, but something stopped her. She really needed to get to the ceremony. Not to mention that these chambers belonged to the saperes and she had no business going inside. With an irritated shake of her head, she started moving forward again. There was another growl. This time, accompanied with the clattering of metal. Then a whine, followed by a whimper. It had to be an animal of some sort, and she felt its agony. What was going on?

She really had to get to the ceremony.

She tried to move forward again, but her feet wouldn't move beneath her. She knocked her palms against her thighs as if that would get her going again. She swiveled to stare at the closed door before her. It was most likely locked and she'd never get in. She tried the handle. Sure enough it was locked. She heard the growl again. It faded out to a cry for help. Reila stood there looking at the locked door, wishing she could get inside but knowing that wishes would not unbolt the door.

She really, really had to get to the titling ceremony.

She took a couple steps away from the door, but then heard a click behind her. The sound made her turn back. The door, now unlocked, creaked opened.

"Hello?" she called out tentatively.

When she got no response, she pushed the door slightly more open and looked inside. In the room, there was a chair near what appeared to be a rather large, but empty cage. A bookshelf stood against the far left wall. She didn't see anything that could've been making the sound.

She really, really, really needed to be getting to the ceremony.

Maybe the creature she heard had gotten out of the cage. Certainly a sapere wouldn't want his pet out roaming around, especially if it were hurt. She would check to see if she could find it, put it back if she did, close the door behind her if she couldn't. Reila walked in the room. She saw no animal. Curious, she went to the bookshelf to see if there were any clues about what kind of creature may have been in the cage or what she should be looking for. The shelves contained several texts about dragons, books on different kinds, their care, and the ritual for each sapere for their dragon. She knew that the saperes' temple held more tomes than this, but this was certainly a varied and interesting collection. What was it doing in here?

The rattling sounded again, making Reila jump. She spun around fully expecting to find something behind her. But the room was still empty.

Then she heard the growl again.

There was definitely something in the room which she could not see.

"Hello?" she called out again. She didn't have magic and so couldn't feel any around her, but that didn't stop her nerves from twinging under her skin and rising with goose bumps as she looked around. Something was in the room with her. If she listened, she could hear him breathing. No, it was breathing, but she was pretty certain it wasn't human.

"Let me out of this cage," a deep voice rumbled.

She felt compelled to move to the cage as if it had her wrapped in a spell. She really should have gone to the ceremony. "Who are you?" she called out desperately. "I can't see you."

A shimmer rippled inside the cage and Reila saw a fledgling dragon appear. Even for as young as it was, it had to curl tightly around within the cage. No wonder it was so angry when it could barely lift its head. Its scales sparkled in a multitude of colors from the light coming through the window.

Reila found herself staring at the dragon. "You are so beautiful," she muttered, the words slurred together as if she were talking in her sleep.

Without fear, she reached through the bars and touched the creature's twinkling scales near what she figured to be its shoulder. The dragon made as if to turn, which pressed its body against her palm.

With a panicked gasp, the dragon stepped backwards, running into the bars behind it. It watched her with glistening black eyes. "I shouldn't be trapped in here," it cried out. No longer was its voice deep and scary, but rather small and frightened.

"No," she agreed with it. Her hand reached to the latch on the cage.

She pulled the pin out.

The dragon rushed out of the cage, knocking the door back, which caught Reila's arm between the bars. As Reila cried out in pain, she saw the dragon shimmer once more and disappear as it headed for the open door.

She clutched her battered arm to her chest. "Ow," she muttered, rubbing the sore spot. "That's gratitude for you."

Still massaging her injury, Reila left the room. Her soreness was probably nothing compared to the reprimand she'd receive if the saperes found out she had released the dragon from its cage. She wondered how long it would be. Since the dragon was invisible, would they discover it was missing before she left for the Ch'bauldi temple. It served the saperes right for keeping a dragon caged up.

What if there had been a reason for the dragon to be caged? What if it were insane?

She tried to recall what kind it had been. She remembered the colors flashing on its scales, but couldn't say that she knew what type of dragon had multicolors like that.

"Reila," a deep voice called to her. "Come on already!"

Reila looked up to see Traese standing at the door to the main hall waving his arms frantically.

"We've been waiting," he snapped as she arrived there. Beyond Traese stood Sapere Juliac with a very grumpy look on his aged face.

"I'm sorry," she said, wishing she had something more to

offer in explanation for her tardiness, but she hadn't even had duties at the shrine this morning.

They moved from the doorway to admit her to the room. Rows of people-filled chairs lined the aisle all the way up to a podium where the Grand Sapere stood with a tall staff in hand. The look on his face seemed to mirror what she'd seen on both Traese's and Juliac's faces. All the other saperes about to be titled stood against the wall by the door. Several of them rolled their eyes and sneered at her.

Every eyeball in the audience seemed to turn to look at her as she entered and Reila suddenly felt very self-conscious. She tried to smile an apology.

"Sorry, everyone," she whispered to her classmates, though she certainly didn't feel it in her heart. If she held up their graduation, it served them right for the teasings they had doled out to her in steady increments over the years. Suddenly, she wished she'd not only come in here later, but muddy and laughing as well. What need did she have to apologize to them? Tomorrow, she would be on her own way to start her own life.

Fortunately, she saw Lon stick his foot out before she tripped over it. "Real mature," she muttered at him as she took her place in line.

"So is showing up on time," he responded.

Musicians began to play from where they sat behind the Grand Sapere. The line of soon-to-be saperes began to walk slowly down the aisle. People clapped and cheered for their initiate. Reila felt a moment of pride until she remembered that there was no one out there cheering for her. Yes, the Keepers from the shrine were happy for her, but they had had their celebration for her yesterday and none could take the time from their duties to be here today. The Dragon Council had privately congratulated her last night at the shrine and would not do so now publicly. Her parents had both died in the mines, as was the short life expectancy of workers who went into the debtors' mine. Reila wished she could walk away from the ceremony, but she was already next in line.

She watched as the Grand Sapere passed the staff with a carved dragon head to Lon. Lon turned it in a circle, then handed it back to the Grand Sapere. Lon had now opened up a symbolic doorway into the dragon realm. Lon stepped forward over the imaginary threshold he had created. The Grand Sapere placed a hand on Lon's shoulder. Then Lon went to stand off to the left side.

Something nibbled on Reila's hair, making her jump backwards. She reached up to her head, but felt nothing there.

The Grand Sapere beckoned Reila forward.

Reila stepped up before the Grand Sapere. "Congratulations," he said as he handed her the staff.

At least she felt like he meant the word and she gave him a smile. She really hoped she made it out of here before the saperes noticed the dragon was out of its cage. She hefted the staff, surprised at the heavy weight of it in her hands. She made the circle before her, then handed the staff back to the Grand Sapere.

As she went to step forward over the pretend threshold line that she'd created, something nudged her shoulder and she stumbled forward. The Grand Sapere caught her arm.

"Easy now," he said. "Are you all right?"

From both in front and from behind her, Reila heard snickering and she was transported back through time to all the days when her classmates had laughed at her. "I'm fine," she lied as she righted herself.

The Grand Sapere placed his hand on her shoulder to bestow the blessing of becoming a sapere upon her. Something knocked Reila's other shoulder, pushing her against the Grand Sapere's palm. His eyes widened.

"I'm sorry," Reila muttered. "I don't know what that is."

Reila got shoved forward again, this time into the Grand Sapere. He nearly dropped his staff as they stumbled a step backward together. Now it was Reila's turn to put her hands on his shoulders as she pushed herself back and regained her balance. "I'm sorry," she repeated.

Once again, her braid was being tugged. She tried to turn her head, but something had a tight grip on her braid. Then, the munching began.

"It's eating my hair," she yelled.

Someone in the audience screamed. Then someone else, followed by another.

Reila turned far enough around that she saw people getting up out of their chairs. Several people looked back over their shoulders as they hurried down the aisle.

Then she saw what had a hold of her hair. The shimmering dragon.

The dragon head of the carved staff appeared over her shoulder as the Grand Sapere thrust it toward the dragon. "Back, foul beast," he screamed.

That wasn't going to be enough. She just knew it. Reila reached up and grabbed her braid. With a tug, she pulled it from the dragon's teeth. The end of it had been gnawed off completely. "What are you doing?" she said in the best chiding tone that she could when she really wanted to shriek in fear.

The dragon finished chewing and swallowed. He looked at the wooden stick the Grand Sapere held toward him and pulled back his lips as if it was going to use the staff as a toothpick. "Thank you. Just what I needed," the dragon said.

The Grand Sapere, looking thoroughly displeased, yanked his staff back and slammed the end of it against the floor.

Sapere Juliac stepped in front of the Grand Sapere. "Who let you out?"

The dragon looked coyly at the ceiling. "I don't know. Might've been fairies."

Now that the saperes had everyone out of the room, one came back in carrying a rather large stick with a loop of rope on the end of it. He walked across the floor on his tip toes and Reila wondered why he would carry on in such a form. She was certain that the dragon could not only hear him, but smell him as well. One did not just sneak up on a dragon. All too often, as she now well knew, it was the other way around.

"Well, beast, it's time to get back in your cage," Sapere Juliac said.

The dragon growled. "My name is Stardust." He swung his head toward the sapere coming toward him and exhaled a thick ribbon of steam in his direction, making the Sapere jump back with a yike. "I have no desire to go back to that cage," the dragon said.

"The point is not up for negotiations and you are not a dragon."

"He looks like a dragon to me," Reila said as she stepped up beside the dragon and took its face in her hands.

The Grand Sapere grabbed her wrist and dragged her away. "Believe me, that is no dragon."

"Then what is it?" she asked.

"We don't know. It is not listed in any book of dragon types," Sapere Juliac responded.

"Could it be a new breed then?" she asked, her fascination and her imagination running away with her mouth before she had a chance to think through the question.

"It's not a new breed," the Grant Sapere scoffed. "That is quite impossible."

Reila felt that that was exactly what was going on in the circumstance. "He is," she insisted. "He's a shimmer dragon."

The Grand Sapere looked taken aback.

Stardust stretched up on his front legs a little bit and

rolled his front shoulders proudly, puffing out his chest a little bit. His head raised, his chin tipping upward. "That's right. I'm a shimmer dragon. And my name is Stardust."

"Now look what you've done, girl," the Grand Sapere snapped. "You should leave now. First you're late for the ceremony, and then you cause this disruption before you can even be titled."

"I stepped through the threshold. You put your hand on my shoulder. I am now a sapere." She would not let her title be taken from her just because this beast had decided to follow her in here. So far, she couldn't really be linked to releasing this beast. There was no way this could be her responsibility, yet.

"That's right," Stardust shouted. "I want her for my sapere. Her hair tastes very good."

And she had once worried about novihomidraks eating her! Now she had a hungry shimmer dragon wanting her as a sapere and to eat her hair. So far, she was off to a spiffy start as a sapere.

"She can't be your sapere. She is going off to be..." The Grand Sapere said, but as he lost track of his words, he looked at Reila and asked, "What kind of dragon were you going to go serve?"

"Ch'bauldi," Reila replied flatly as she stared at Stardust.

"Yes, yes, she's going to serve the Ch'bauldi dragons. She's going to be their sapere."

"I am a dragon," Stardust shouted. "I want her for my sapere."

"But she can't be," the Grand Sapere continued to refute Stardust.

Stardust opened his mouth and blew his breath in Reila's direction. She raised her hands, using her forearms to guard her face, as it felt like she was being pelted in a sandstorm. She wanted to cry out, but she didn't dare open her mouth. Who knew what this Dragon was spewing at her?

After several intense seconds, it stopped. Reila still didn't lower her arms.

"There. I have marked her as my own." Stardust seemed quite pleased with himself.

"Reila?" Sapere Juliac asked as he reached out, but did not touch Reila.

Reila now lowered her arms and opened her eyes to see Stardust grinning while Sapere Juliac and the Grand Sapere looked horrified. She wondered if the dragon had sandblasted her skin right off of her. Was she nothing but a bloody mass now? But before she even looked down, Stardust gave a little wiggle and said, "I marked her as my sapere."

Reila looked down at her arms, and saw little sparkling flecks covering her skin. What had just happened to her?

"Go," Sapere Juliac whispered to the Grand Sapere, who began to slink off along the wall until he felt himself far enough away to escape and began running.

Sapere Juliac stepped toward her, once again reaching out, but not quite touching her. "Reila, are you okay?"

Reila drew back to keep Sapere Juliac from touching her. She wasn't sure if she was okay or not. To look at her arms, it seemed as if thousands of shards of glass were piercing her skin and reflecting prisms of light. Yet there was no actual pain. She looked to Stardust. She licked her dry lips, and felt some of the grit roll across her tongue. She wanted to spit or wipe her tongue against her arm, but she figured both those possibilities would just make this worse. "What have you done to me," she whispered.

Stardust tilted his head as if she'd asked her question in a completely foreign language. His eyes filled with concern. "Did you not want to be my sapere?" he queried.

"I..." If this was how all dragons marked the children that they chose to be Sapere's, she was really glad it hadn't happened sooner. Or maybe, the incident was better lost along with all the other childhood memories that one loses in their early years.

"I'm sorry. I had to do it so fast. It was my first time," Stardust said, his voice frosted with sadness. "He made me do it."

"Did not!" Sapere Juliac protested.

"I'm fine," Reila lied. "I just... I think I'll go take a shower." All she could think about was that if she'd been out in an ordinary sandstorm, she'd want to take a shower. It didn't look like the flecks were actually stuck to her skin, but just needed washed off. She hoped that was the reality of the situation.

"Just shake it off." Stardust himself made the motion like a shaking dog. "See? That easy."

Somehow, Reila didn't figure it would be quite as easy for her, but she began to shake and twitch her limbs in an effort to shake off the flecks. She felt a multitude of them fall away from her. A few battered the floor with a light tinkling sound. Most of them she felt hit against her dress.

"There. Ohh, doesn't she look pretty?" Stardust said.

Reila opened her eyes to see Sapere Juliac still staring at her with utter horror. She wished she knew what was so wrong with her appearance. She looked down at herself but couldn't see anything wrong. The flecks that had once stuck in her skin like little shards of glass had fallen away but around the tattoo brand, the black ink now sparkled beautifully like a true sapere's brand.

Sapere Juliac stammered as he started to move sideways, his eyes still wide with terror. He looked as though he was judging the distance between them, to see if she could reach out and grab him still, and when he felt he was a safe enough distance away that she couldn't reach him, he turned and fled the room.

"Stardust, what's wrong with me?" she asked.

"Nothing. You have been made my sapere, nothing more. I'm so excited, are you?"

Reila still felt like there was something wrong, that she was missing something. She could hear the Grand Sapere and Sapere Juliac in the hallway hurriedly speaking to other saperes and urging them down the hall away from this room. She thought she heard something about defile the sanctuary as well. For some reason they thought her a demon.

Reila took the side door out of the temple and walked over to the courtyard fountain. She looked down to find her own reflection held within the pool. Her brown hair now glistened, shimmering in that same strange way that Stardust's dragon scales did. And her eyes... She hadn't realized that she'd gotten the grit in her eyes, but obviously she had. They had the same multicolor illusion as Stardust's; black beneath, but shimmering and sparkling on top. It was the intensity of those eyes which now stared back at her that she knew Sapere Juliac had feared. Even as she stared down at herself trying to adjust to the idea that these were going to be her new eyes, she had to wonder if she could see into the souls of others and wondered if Sapere Juliac had also pondered the same thing.

"They will never accept me now," Reila said. "I am truly an oddity."

"As if I am any different," Stardust said. "If you look beneath the mask which everyone wears, you will find that we are all oddities. That's what makes each of us unique."

"Why have you done this to me?"

"You freed me and now I have freed you. You put your imprint on me when you touched me and called me beautiful, and I have placed my magic upon you,"

"But I have no magic."

"You will need it.

"Why?"

"I have done what dragons do: I have chosen you. Moonhunter, after he finishes his apprenticeship, will be my guardian. I selected him a long time ago. I want you to be my sapere, my Grand Sapere," Stardust said in a voice much more mature than he'd used previously. Then he smiled. "What more could there possibly be?"

She took another long look at the reflection of herself in the fountain, Stardust looking over her shoulder. For just a moment, it felt right to be here with Stardust. "Moonhunter once told me I was kissed by the Onesong, though I didn't realize it yet. This was the moment he'd been talking about."

"What else did he teach you that night?"

"That everyone's life adventure is unique." She realized as she looked up into the dragon's amazing eyes, a reflection of her own, that they so obviously belonged to one another now. "He reminded me to stay open and curious, to never close down any possibilities."

"Are you ready to go, to begin our next adventure?"

"I certainly am."

Stardust helped Reila get up on his back. They headed to the stone columns at the center of the garden where the convergence to the Wells opened.

"You will do the honors?" Stardust asked.

It seemed like there had never been a time when she didn't know the spell. Reila cast the magic to open the Wells.

READY FOR ANOTHER QUEST?

Sign up for Dawn Blair's newsletter to learn about new releases, get access to fun and free stuff, hear about events, and more!

It's easy.

Go to **WWW.DAWNBLAIR.COM/NEWSLETTER** to join the adventure and get a free PDF of the reading order to Dawn's books.

WHEN HELPING A PRINCESS TO FIND THREE LOST BOOKS,
HE NEVER EXPECTED TO MAKE SUCH ENEMIES.

The courage to become legendary.

Discover the magic in the epic fantasy adventure of the
Sacred Knight series

Start the series with Quest for the Three Books
Get your copy at www.morningskystudios.com
or your favorite bookstore.

LOKI, NORSE GOD OF MISCHIEF, IS HERE TO SAVE
HUMANITY. MAYBE. IF HE FEELS LIKE IT.

CLICK TO GET YOUR COPY NOW!

https://books2read.com/1-800-callloki/

Dawn Blair grew up on a ranch in a rural Nevada town. The old buildings provided inspiration for her imagination as she thrived on stories of unicorns, princesses, heroic knights, and hidden doors to other dimensions.

For as long as she can remember, Dawn has had a passion for storytelling. Though she started out writing, her creative life expanded into painting and illustration.

She loves creating worlds and spinning tales for people to enjoy. The best ones are the stories that surprise her as she's writing. She loves her characters doing the unexpected. She'll gladly tell you that the most exciting part about being a writer is being the first one on the journey.

Thank you for taking the time to join her on these adventures.

Find more about Dawn and her work at:
www.dawnblair.com

facebook.com/dawnblairbooks
twitter.com/dawnblair
instagram.com/dawn.blair

Made in the USA
Middletown, DE
10 July 2023

34796838R00086